# THE SECRET BOOKCASE OF

# SHERLOCK HOLMES

# *THE SUPPRESSED MEMOIRS*

## Volume the First

### PRESENTED FOR THE FIRST TIME.

*By Rabbi Dr. Walter Rothschild*

© 

Rabbi Dr. Walter Rothschild

**ISBN:** 9798680620991

## About the Author

Rabbi Dr. Walter Rothschild is a writer, poet, broadcaster and cabaret artist who has worked as a community rabbi in the UK, Aruba, Germany, Poland and Austria. He is a railway historian and an expert on Railways and the Holocaust and also Railways of the Middle East.

Further information about him can be found on:

**www.walterrothschild.de**

**www.rabbiwalterrothschild.de**

**www.rothschild-comedy.de**

**www.harakevet.com**

# Introduction

All those who have carefully read the splendid accounts of Dr. John Watson concerning the intelligence, insight and integrity, the deductive and didactic powers of his erstwhile colleague and friend, Mr. Sherlock Holmes, will be aware that we have, at best, only a small fraction of their story. These two English gentlemen pursue their parallel careers with but occasional mention of domestic matters; Holmes remains a bachelor in a fitting bachelor apartment, suitably convenient for The Regents Park and all the opportunities for a bachelor life that may be offered there. Watson, as a medical man through and through, cannot help but mention from time to time the pharmacological habits of his friend - habits that, though perhaps acceptable at that period, would nowadays earn more than a raised eyebrow. But it was these habits, and the playing of his Stradivarius violin, that helped Holmes to get through some of the deeper periods of his obsessive melancholia. Which is the cause and which is the effect is, at this distance in time and even with the newest psychological insights, hard to determine. His almost erotic obsession with railway timetables has already been well investigated, his scientific and chemical experiments were, alas, never published.

It is clear that there is much that we are not told and for decades scholars have struggled in a vain endeavour to elucidate more of the lives of these gentlemen. Now, through one of those strange serendipital coincidences upon which we so often rely, there has come to light a bundle of yellowing manuscripts in an ancient desk that was being disposed of as the former offices of "Strand Magazine" were being demolished for redevelopment. These stories, it appears, composed and edited from his notes, and then submitted by Dr. Watson according to his usual practice, were in fact suppressed by the then-Editor, as unsuitable for publication. On reading them we can perhaps see why, for they cast our characters in positions of ambiguity and doubt that could be considered to undermine their moral integrity - an integrity upon which so much of their careers relied. Elements of Holmes's youth, background and private tastes are revealed which may shock those readers who had never considered to contemplate that no-one springs, fully-formed and wholly perfect, into this world.

In view of the years that have passed, it is considered that there is no danger in revealing now the contents of these manuscripts. The reader will be left to judge for him or herself whether the more rounded picture which presents itself makes us more or less appreciative of the skills and talents of this remarkable detective.

---

EDITED AND HUMBLY PRESENTED TO THE
READING PUBLIC

BY

## RABBI DR. WALTER ROTHSCHILD

**WARNING**: Not for the Humourless

# Table of Contents

| | |
|---|---|
| The Case of the Spanish Fly | 8 |
| Beating the Habit | 21 |
| The Confused Atheist | 25 |
| Squaring the Circle | 38 |
| The Case of the Horn in the Fog | 51 |
| The Case of the Final Curtain | 56 |
| The Rose of the Names | 69 |
| Death and Taxes | 77 |
| Sherlock, Go Home | 88 |
| The Inseed Job | 92 |
| The Case of the Powdered Milk | 105 |
| The Music Hall Mystery | 108 |
| The Case with the Missing Suit | 114 |

# SHERLOCK HOLMES' BOOKCASE.

## THE CASE OF THE SPANISH FLY

Many is the dark night I have passed with my friend and companion Sherlock Holmes, in pursuit of some evidence of evil. Yet few experiences, I confess, have terrified me quite so much as the period we spent, tramping across Exmoor, in search of the clue to resolve one of the most fiendish and wide-ranging conspiracies I have ever encountered.

As was so often the case, the matter presented itself initially to us as a query from a concerned stranger. Having finished a meagre dinner with one of Mrs. Hudson's dreadful pies and some undercooked potatoes, (my friend often said he could solve almost every problem except that of Mrs. Hudson's cooking), Sherlock and I were considering whether to repair to a hostelry for something a little more refreshing when there was a knock at the door downstairs. A few minutes later a visitor was ushered in.

"Do come in, Señor!" said Sherlock, waving our visitor to the spare armchair before he could speak. "You may take your coat off - you will find it much warmer here than in the Pyrenees, I vouchsafe. And cleaner, too. I understand Bilbao can be rather muddy at this season."

"But what... I mean, how on earth?" gasped or stammered our guest, near speechless with shock.

"Do not be dismayed, Señor" said Sherlock. "It is really nothing special. Your suit has a Spanish cut to it, your moustache likewise, you wear a small pin upon your lapel which indicates you belong to a learned society of Iberian historians, and the mud upon your trouser turn-ups has that rather peculiar shade of yellowish-reddish-brown that I have, until now, discovered only along the northern coast of your country, from El Ferrol and westwards. And you are clearly dressed warmly as though for a mountain crossing, although it is as yet only early autumn."

"My country! My country! But that is the issue on which I have come to see you, Señor Chol-mess."(For so he pronounced the name of my friend.) "My country is under threat, and my Government has sent me to you, to beg for your help."

"Tell me more," said Sherlock, sitting back and taking out his pipe. "Does this have anything to do with the Hounds of Hell?"

Our visitor was visibly impressed. "Just an educated guess," said Sherlock. "I have, of course, been following news of the conflict in 'The Times'. As I understand it, there is a group of conspirators who are agitating to detach the northern part of Spain from the rest of the Kingdom and establish their own independent Basque Republic, and they appear prepared to commit any outrage to achieve their ends?"

"But that is it, exactly!" said our visitor. "Allow me to present myself formally. I am Don Cortez y Jeromias y Maria y Valesquista, of my country's Foreign Service, and my mission is, indeed, a delicate one. We have received certain informations that a group of these, these rebels, are meeting here, in England, to plan their outrages. It is here that they prepare, and here even that they may obtain some of their explosives, either from sympathisers or from other, less discerning but more commercial sources. But we do not know where. Nor can Scotland Yard assist us in this, and even your own Secret Service, I regret to say, has until now been unsuccessful in narrowing down the possible locations. And this is why my Government decided to approach you, Señor Chol-mess, for your reputation has of course spread far and wide."

My friend was gratified at this, so gratified that he almost managed not to wince at the way his name was mangled and mispronounced. "And these are the so-called 'Hounds of Hell'?"

"Si, Seňor. This is one of the code names they use. The more exact translation would be the Hounds of the Devil. Los Perros del Diablo. It is a name designed to strike terror into the hearts of any honest Basque farmers or fishermen. They have shot at policemen and attached bombs to stagecoaches, they have burned down a post office and thrown missiles at civil servants. The entire region is in uproar, and we seek any means - I repeat, Mr. Chol-mess - ANY means - to apprehend these brigands. And, I am sure I do not need to explain myself fully, my Government would of course seek to reward most handsomely your noble efforts on our behalfs." It is hard to bow deeply from an armchair, but no doubt Spanish noblemen and diplomats receive special training in the art.

"I see," said Holmes, thoughtfully stuffing a little more of his special tobacco mixture into his pipe. "Well, if there is any more information you can give us - names, place of last sighting, that sort of thing - then I am sure that my friend Doctor Watson and I would be most gratified to assist in your endeavours."

There were times later, I confess, when I wished he had not involved me so apparently thoughtlessly and carelessly as he did then. By the time our visitor had expressed his effusive thanks and greetings and finally left, it was clearly too late to do much more about getting a decent meal and I left Sherlock sitting in his chair, already on his third pipe - a significant symbol for the difficulties this case was to pose us.

The following morning, I found Sherlock pacing his rooms, showing all the signs of a sleepless night. Several back issues of the 'Times' lay scattered, opened to specific pages, on the table. An Atlas of Great Britain and a current Bradshaw, together with a copy of Thomas Cooks' Timetable for Europe, had also been employed. The overflowing ashtray with its pile of ash told its own story, as did my friend's wild eyes and the crumpled twists of paper of the sort in which certain medications are sometimes informally delivered.

"Aha! Watson! There you are!" he cried. This was hardly Holmes at his best, for I already knew where I was and even who I was, and so no great powers of deduction could have been required. But I held my peace, giving my friend the benefit of the doubt. It had, no doubt, been a long night. "I think I may have a lead," he said. And pulling me to the table he began to point, gesticulate and almost gabble the results of his nocturnal cogitations.

"That Scotland Yard could not help, surprises me not a jot," he said, "But if even our Secret Services are at a loss, then it is a serious matter. Nevertheless, one must return to first principles. As I always maintain, if the improbable cannot be the answer, then we must look to the impossible. So - from where can the North Coast of Spain be most easily reached? Let us assume the borders with France are carefully watched, as also those with Portugal. We are left with the South Coast of Britain, specifically the South-West. Lonely country, plenty of small harbours and inlets, and even an occasional ferry service from Plymouth, but well away from most observers.

Where can explosives be easily obtained? Why, where there are quarries, of course, and Exmoor is littered with them. I am sure our quarry, haha, is to be sought in that region. And, by the way, I am almost certain our visitor last night had been followed or observed. These devilish fellows are too clever to let a Spanish diplomat wander around London on his own, without taking note of where he goes and upon whom he calls. Therefore, we must assume that we, too, could be under suspicion, possibly in danger.

From Bradshaw I see we have a choice of a South-Western train to Exeter and then Padstow, or a Great Western one to Exeter and then, by changing earlier at Taunton, we may reach Barnstaple and then take a local. Since we so often take a train from Paddington, I think this time, for the sake of caution, we shall go to Waterloo. And Watson, I would suggest you pack for two or three days away, bring some warm and waterproof clothing and - do not forget your Army

Revolver! Be back here within the hour, for time, tide and the South-Western waits for no man."

In this, as it transpired, Holmes was wrong, for the London & South-Western Railway did indeed show little interest in a punctual departure for its crack West of England express and we dallied in Waterloo for a good fifteen minutes before a figure could be spied running from the buffer stops towards the train, which promptly whistled and then steamed its way out of the station. Holmes, who had been leaning out of the window and giving me a commentary, was thoughtful as he settled back in our First-Class compartment. "Strange," he observed, "that the Express waited for someone who appeared to be wearing workmen's clothing and carrying a bag of what appeared to be quarrying tools. Yet more I could not observe, for he was a good way away." And with that he closed his eyes and began to catch up on some of his lost sleep, exhausted by the mental exertions of the night.

It was several weary hours later and following two changes of train that we climbed out of our carriage at the lonely Halwill Junction. There being but one trap from the village, there was no point in Holmes endeavouring to let the first and second depart before hailing it. He had, however, at each major station, leaned out carefully to see whether a specific person might have left the train.

The choice of accommodation was equally limited but at least the food and liquid refreshments available were much better than those at 221B Baker Street and we quaffed deeply and tucked in as good trenchermen should, before retiring. Yet our sleep was disturbed by some remarkable howling noises from the wild and lonely moor which surrounded the Inn where we lodged. Twice I awoke to find Sherlock sitting up by the window, alert, staring from behind the net curtains into the inky darkness beyond.

In the morning it was clear that the ravages of the night had done his mood no good, yet we tucked into our breakfasts with an appetite sharpened by the cool fresh air.

The next two days were spent, under the thin guise of geological prospecting and searching for fossils - a topic on which we spoke loudly at mealtimes, for all to overhear - clambering over various windswept Tors and through waterlogged bogs, returning each evening to our Inn. And each night I was awakened once more by that unearthly howling, and each time Sherlock would approach the window, cautiously and in such a manner that none outside would perceive him in the darkened room yet stare intently through the net curtains.

On our third morning Sherlock examined carefully the ground around the Inn and especially that section of garden below our window, it having rained slightly during the night. The intentness of his examination was broken by an occasional snort and an expression of satisfaction. "I perceive, Watson, that we are indeed under observation. As I expected." And with that he set off once more to the Moor and refused to answer any questions, devoting himself instead to close examination of three rocky outcrops, which he tapped with a small pocket hammer.

But that evening, after we had returned for an early supper, Holmes suggested we went to have a walk to the station. As the evening Stopper for Exeter pulled into the platform, he wandered over to look at the locomotive. Then he pulled me to him and said quietly, "Watson, my friend, I must ask you to undertake a very special and urgent journey. Look casual and look at the locomotive. In one minute, this train will depart. Once it starts, jump quickly on board. It doesn't matter that you have no ticket - you can sort that out at Exeter. Once there, go straight to the Police Station and hand the officer in charge this letter."

So saying, he took from his jacket pocket an envelope - I could swear that I had not seen him writing anything that entire day, my face must have registered as such for he said "Do not worry. I wrote this last night, while you were asleep, in case my suspicions were to be confirmed. I cannot send a telegram from here - it would be read. Instead, Watson, you must, from Exeter, also cable to Lestrade at the Yard to come down here as soon as possible with a squad of the best men he can find in the time available. Everything else is in the letter."

The guard whistled, the locomotive whistled, I whistled - with astonishment. "Quick, now, Watson!" he urged, "So quickly that no-one can follow you. We must take them by surprise!" And so saying he grabbed a door handle, opened the door, thrust me into a compartment and slammed it shut, turning away as wreaths of steam hid him from my sight!

With a turmoil of emotions, I slumped into a seat, barely noticing it was only Second-Class. I was on my way to deliver a vital message and yet my friend was left totally alone in the face of great and unknown dangers! But there was little I could do except to carry out his wishes. With anxiety I opened the envelope and scanned the contents, the enormity of what was written therein driving me yet further back into my seat and away from the window.

My train reached Exeter Central at almost midnight, after a spasmodic ascent of the steep gradient from St. David's, but following the advice contained in the letter I threw a gold sovereign at the ticket collector and ran out of the station, avoiding all cabs. The first policeman I saw directed me to the main Police Station, and here I presented myself - admittedly by now a little disheveled and breathless - at the Night Desk and asked to see the Superintendent in charge. When this personage appeared, disturbed by my urgent cries as the officers attempted to detain me for being Disorderly, I handed him the letter.

Matters moved quickly from this point; Telegrams were sent, messages written and delivered by hand, and after a short and restless night spent in a cell, where at least I could stretch out and sleep fitfully, the Superintendent, accompanied by ten sturdy Constables, accompanied me back to Central Station. There we awaited the arrival of the early-morning so-called 'Milk Train', actually the Mail and Newspaper Express from London since the milk, of course, is transported from Devon to London and not the other way around. To our enormous relief, leaning out of a window in the rear coach was our old friend Inspector Lestrade, who was travelling with five further gentlemen, all in civilian clothing. We embarked with him and learned that, so far as he could tell, there had been no suspicious additional travellers at Waterloo. It appeared that secrecy had been maintained. But what of Holmes? My thoughts bore bitterly upon me as our train ploughed conscientiously through the Devon countryside in the rising morning, until at last we disembarked - from different compartments along the length of the remaining three carriages - at Halwill Junction.

Swiftly Superintendent Jawnson and nine of his men occupied the Station Master's Office and the Telegraph Office, to ensure that no word of our arrival should percolate through to others along the line. One Constable remained upon the locomotive as far as Padstow, to ensure that no messages were sent by the locomotive driver and fireman. I set out to the Inn, with Lestrade and his party following at discreet intervals - these were professional Secret Service men, and yet protective cover was sadly lacking in so inhospitable a place.

At the Inn there was no sign of Holmes, but when we forced our way into the room which we had so recently shared it showed signs of struggle and of a hasty departure. Bedding lay upon the floor, Holmes' tobacco pouch lay still on the dresser - I searched hastily and with sinking heart for clues, for a message, but could find nothing unusual apart from a small bottle of red, hot Tabasco sauce. This I showed to Lestrade and Jawnson, who were as mystified as myself.

The Innkeeper, who professed at first no knowledge of anything untoward, was taken into custody in his own premises. The Inspector, the Secret Service men and I set forth onto the Moor, searching for a trail. Here and there, indeed, we could trace the passage of footsteps, the dragging of a person, some broken twigs, and similar subtleties which only the trained eyes could perceive. The trail brought us to the lip of a small quarry and to a pathway leading down into it, where - now throwing caution to the winds and moving as fast as we dared down the escarpment - we made our way to a wooden barrack hut. A shout showed that we had been observed, a further stream of curses in some strange foreign language followed, and a shot rang out - but to our great good fortune, not one of our men was hurt and we surrounded the barrack, taking cover from any sight through the windows. "Come out!" called Lestrade in a stentorian voice. "Come out! You are surrounded! Further resistance is useless! Throw down your weapons and come out!"

Mutterings and oaths were heard from within, but then the door slowly opened and three men reluctantly emerged, dressed in quarrymen's overalls. They were lined up against the wall of the barrack and I rushed inside. "Holmes, Holmes!" I cried. "You called?" replied a familiar voice from a dark corner. I picked up a lamp and, lo, it was indeed my good friend Sherlock, bound with ropes to a chair and looking somewhat bruised. He had, it appeared, put up a good and honourable fight when abducted. One side of the barrack was filled to the ceiling with packages that were clearly of an explosive nature.

Within the hour the three had been placed, together with the Innkeeper and the Station Master, into the locked Luggage Office of the station, guarded by some of the sturdy Constables, and the search was on for other members of the plot. Lestrade, at Holmes' suggestion, refrained from summoning a special train for the prisoners as this might merely have alarmed a senior railway official elsewhere along the line. Instead it was agreed that all those scooped into the bag thus far would be quietly escorted in the luggage van of the next up train. And that very afternoon Holmes and I caught the London Express.

Two days later Lestrade came, as previously arranged, to call. He brought with him a package and Don Cortez y Jeromias y Maria y Valesquista, who was naturally more than effusive and who also brought a package with him. We left the packages unopened until later - Holmes' tastes were already widely known - but opened with alacrity one of the bottles of fine Jerez sherry which our visitor had also taken from his case and took, each of us, several glasses. And only then did we take the opportunity to enquire of my friend the process of deduction that had led to the rounding-up of such a dangerous gang of brigands.

Sitting back in his armchair, Holmes slowly filled his pipe whilst Inspector Lestrade, Don Cortez y Jeromias y Maria y Valesquista and I waited with barely restrained impatience. He appeared to be relishing our discomfiture.

"It was, of course, quite elementary, once the fog of confusion had been lifted. The Basque people wish to distance themselves from the rest of Spain and consider that the blood of the Spaniards has been contaminated by the Arabs who conquered and dominated the Iberian Peninsula for so long. They hate and despise the Moors, as they are termed. This also led me to think that "Ex-Moor" might be a symbolically significant area in which to store and hoard their weapons and explosives. In Devon, of course, and especially around Plymouth, the hatred of the Spaniard dates back to Drake's time and any group of brigands that seeks to 'singe the Spanish beard' once again may well receive a cautious but warm welcome.

So, the question was Where to start? Here, I confess, I had some initial doubts, but nevertheless consider it fortuitous that I chose the South-Western line that day. You will, by the way, recall, Lestrade, that on the very day we travelled there was a fracas at Paddington in which a certain unfortunate gentleman wearing a deerstalker and sou-wester and carrying a cane was set upon and injured by a bunch of ruffians? The 'Times' reported briefly on the incident. Ironically, it was while considering whether to take a 'sou-wester' that I determined to travel down from Waterloo instead. Even so, you will recall, Watson, that someone in a position of authority on that Line was enabled to hold back the main express until one of the band, complete with his working clothes and tools, had arrived to join the very train on which we had been observed.

I too have my powers of observation and noted that he did not detrain until we, too, descended to the platform at Halwill Junction - and yet he disappeared from off the end of the platform, not coming to the normal point for the collection of tickets."

"I didn't see him!" I expostulated.

"Yes, my point precisely," observed Holmes, drily. "If I may continue? The question for me was now, not <u>whether</u> there were certain secret sympathisers with the Basque cause amongst the population, but <u>how many</u>, and <u>where.</u> It was, you will recall, a matter of no choice as to which cab we took and where we might lodge. So, I was pretty sure that those following us knew immediately where we were and would keep us under surveillance. Each night, of course, the watchers and their superiors would communicate with each other with those canine howls - they do refer to themselves, do they not, as the 'Hounds of the Devil'? - and try as I might, I found it near impossible to gain a sight of one of these men, dressed in black as they were, hiding in the darkness of the night and on the moor. But it was clear that we should have to do a little exploring. I assumed from the outset that every step we took would be observed, and my main concern was merely the extent of the reaction we might expect to arouse if we stumbled a little too closely upon their secret.

In consequence I took care to espy the land as widely as I dared - under the pretence of searching for various forms of fossils in the limestone.

I deduced that in such countryside a band of men speaking Spanish or whatever local regional dialect is preferred would soon prove noticeable. However, one or two, working in a quarry, might pass by relatively inconspicuously. Nevertheless, this would imply that the locals were much more involved in the plot than even the foreign visitors, for total secrecy would be impossible and there had to be several local inhabitants in on the plot. But I assumed they would nevertheless have only a subordinate role. So, who could be the ringleader, the contact man to the rebels in Spain itself?

I took a great chance in sending you, Watson, away that evening, but it was clearly necessary to call for reinforcements and at the same time I did not know whether I could trust the Station Master or anyone else here in this forsaken hamlet. I need not remind you that someone senior in the Railway Company appeared to be able to deflect the timetables at will. I could only hope that, despite the telegraph message that might be sent along the line ahead of you, you could manage to get safely to Exeter, escape from the station and get to someone in authority. And then, alone, it was clear to me what I had to do. To beard the lion in his den, so to speak. To lay a trap. But they were too quick for me. I was still alone in the bedroom, preparing some clues for any eventuality, when the door was rudely opened, and three men entered. I put up some resistance, naturally, but" - he touched his left cheek where the bruise was now fading - "it was clear from the outset that the odds were against me. All I could do was to ruffle things up a bit and leave a bottle of Tabasco where you would hopefully find it."

"But what was that meant to mean?" I asked, puzzled.

Holmes gave an exasperated sigh, somewhat exaggeratedly I thought, and replied, "It was to indicate that the Basque had taken me. And the Sauce indicated that the quarry we had visited that day was the source of the explosives."

"Aha!" I said, now satisfied.

"So I was taken, rather roughly I might add, to the place where you fortunately found me - I had done what I could to leave as clear a trail as possible. There I was questioned, also rather roughly, by the ringleader. The man with the reddish hair. For he is the contact man, the only one in fact who has come here from Spain. We do not yet know how far the Ring spreads - there are certainly others here in London - but the others involved at Exmoor are all mere locals who have been recruited to the cause, some with financial inducements, others with - as I have indicated - an appeal to the Englishman's natural and historical aversion to the Spaniard. I apologise, Don Cortez y Jeromias y Maria y Valesquista, but so it is." Our guest nodded graciously in acknowledgement of the apology.

"Well, they may no doubt be released once they have learned their lesson. For a while they had their childish but menacing fun, gathering gunpowder in their huts, howling around the moors at night and pretending to be demonic dogs fighting desperate dagoes. But he - Senor Raxx - he is the dangerous one, and we have done a good day's work indeed in removing him from circulation for some time to come."

"You mean...?" I asked.

"Yes, Watson. He, and he alone, was the Basque of the Hound-Devils."

---------------------------------------------

## **BEATING THE HABIT**

As you may have gathered from some of my earlier accounts, my good friend Sherlock Holmes was wont, on occasion, to partake of a small amount of Cocaine - in order to assist his mental processes. This was a habit that I, as a medical man, did not encourage, yet I saw - at the time - no reason to prevent it. At that time, you must understand, some of the evil side-effects of this medication were not yet fully known and the fact that his eyes occasionally turned blue and he slavered and dribbled from time to time were phenomena I merely put down to that unfortunate occasion when he got too close to the Hound on Dartmoor and bit the wretched beast before it could bite him. (This is an incident which I deliberately omitted from my account of that Case, as it might have upset animal-loving readers. But now, I feel, it can be told.)

But the time drew near when Society came to frown upon my friend's innocent pursuit and it became necessary, should he wish to persist in it, for him to conceal his habit. On the one hand this posed no great problem for one of his intellect and talents at disguise and subterfuge; On the other, it was true that we did indeed travel a great deal at this period in pursuit of various schemes of the devilish Dr. Moriarty and his henchmen. The world needed our constant concern and attention, though it rarely even knew of our exploits on its behalf, and we spent so much time on the ferries from Dover that .... well, I am perhaps getting a little ahead of my tale.

But the fact is that the Customs Agents on both sides of the Channel became aware of our frequent travels, whether to Boulogne or Ostend, and had developed their suspicions. We found ourselves, despite the dreadful hurry in which we often travelled, desperate to get to Paris or Brussels before yet another scandal could break over yet another missing Treaty, having our Gladstone Bags emptied and our carpet bags thoroughly searched, until on one occasion at Calais we even found ourselves missing the Boat Train and having to take instead an 'Omnibus' train via Longeau. And yet, even clouds have a silver lining, for this was the day on which the Paris Boat Express was derailed near Deauville by the dreadful henchmen of our implacable enemy, and it was fortunate indeed that we were not on the train which plunged deep into that hellish ravine. Being on a train on a different route, we knew nothing of this disaster until we reached Paris late that night and were able to purchase the evening newspaper. How we counted our blessings!

I have mentioned that clouds often have silver linings and the same at this point applied to Holmes' large Gladstone, which indeed possessed a lining which, when carefully detached, revealed - if not silver, then at least white powder. But my friend was - though he would not admit it - shaken by this incident. It was one thing to let the first and second hansom cabs go by before taking the third - such a manoeuvre was not always possible with the South-Eastern Railway Company's Channel steamers.

And it was then that he determined to find a yet safer way to transport the substances he required for his regular relaxation. Even I was not told at first, for - of course - the less I knew, the less I could reveal. But one day, much, much later than the incidents I have been describing, when he was one evening in a mellow mood, Mrs. Hudson had taken away the dinner things and he had finished his first post-prandial pipe, the fire glowed in the grate and the noise of the traffic in Baker Street was shut out by those thick curtains, he told me with quiet pride of how he had been able to import substantial amounts of powder to England despite the attentions of the Customs Agents at Dover.

"You will recall, dear Watson," he began, "the Case of the Counterfeit Cheese?" I did indeed - for this was one of those famous occasions when my friend's analytical mind had penetrated a scheme of fraud so great, it had threatened almost the entire Cheese industry of our peaceful neighbours, the Dutch. But once he had demonstrated that the famous so-called "Edam" cheeses were in fact little more than balls of fat wrapped in red wax as a marketing ploy - that this cheese was actually, as its very name implied in devilish code, "Made backwards" in order to gain subsidies from the Milk and Cheese Production Boards - the grateful Dutch had been sending, through their Ambassador in London, regular monthly supplies of "Old Gouda" ever since.

"It was during my investigations in that case that I first met Hendrik van Leerdam, in Amsterdam," he continued. "Hendrik proved to be a valuable assistant (though there is, of course, no need for you to be too concerned, Watson), and once the case had been solved, he showed me a little of his fair city. I was profoundly impressed. The Dutch, it is clear, live very much under the water level - hence their need to wear wooden clogs, which would float should the dykes ever suffer damage - but at the same time they have managed to evolve a way of living which, while very different from ours, has its advantages. In Amsterdam I found whole streets, whole areas devoted to various forms of relaxation. And there were also suppliers able and willing to send whatever one required, at - of course - a price.

I made some enquiries and discovered that there was an efficient and complex network of couriers who were able to travel across Europe at will, with small amounts of whatever one wished concealed upon or even within their person. But no-one would tell me how they did it, and as I was so intrigued, I devoted a couple of days to solving this problem. I was under some slight handicap in terms of their language, of course - a good Englishman of breeding is taught from an early age not to clear his throat constantly in public whilst speaking, yet it is this act which seems to constitute a good two-thirds of Dutch conversation - but eventually I was able to determine the '*modus operandi*'."

I was intrigued and astonished and said so.

"Well, Watson, in the end it was comparatively simple.

The powders in question are sewn carefully into small sachets, which the courier simply swallows. The courier then travels by canal to wherever there is a rendezvous and upon - harrumph - upon evacuating this sachet, and of course washing it then thoroughly in the canal, the product in question can change hands and the customer can be satisfied. It was, in fact, the issue of canals that led me to the answer. To reach England, of course, one must also take a ship, but since the good Hollanders also refer to our English Channel as a "Kanal", this does not disturb the basic underlying principle."

"In what way?" I enquired, thoroughly intrigued by now.

"Well, the courier travels by canal, because that is a slow but safe mode of passage and arouses but little suspicion. And the sachet also travels by canal, albeit by a different one."

"How can this be?" I asked, puzzled. "How could this be, if the sachet in question was inside a person already? What canal could it take?"

Holmes smiled quietly to himself, then said to me, almost gently,

"Alimentary, my dear Watson."

---

# THE CASE OF THE CONFUSED ATHEIST

It was, as usual, a dim autumnal afternoon when the sound of feet on the stairs and a knock at the door indicated the arrival of another visitor. Holmes glanced up from his paper and asked me to open the door. A shabby gentleman of nondescript middle-aged appearance, rather wild eyes and poorly combed hair entered the room. Little did we know that this occasion was to plunge us into terrible conflict with the Forces of Evil, dangers so terrible that, even now, I - but I digress.

"Mr. Holmes?" he asked, clasping his hands in a manner reminiscent of genuflection. "Mr. Holmes, I have come a long way to seek your assistance."

"So I should say," agreed my friend, glancing up from the sports results. "I see you are a minister of religion, of a nonconformist or possibly even of the Hebraic persuasion, from a small and no doubt impoverished parish, deep in the country and some way from a railway station on the South-Eastern Line."

"Why, how in God's name...?" began our visitor, before stopping in awe at his own lack of respect, heresy and profanity.

"It is quite simple," said my friend, in that patronising tone that could be really irritating when applied to oneself but was so fascinating when imposed upon others of lesser wit and intelligence. "Such a dark and drab suit as you wear is commonly worn by vicars of the lesser branches of the Church or ministers of the less significant chapels for I observe you wear no dog-collar; on your right sleeve you still bear traces of wax, indicating that you have to light and clean the candelabra yourself rather than relying upon a caretaker. You have not removed your hat. You have a pronounced twitch in your left eye, a nervous tic often developed by those who have much dealings with Parish Councils.

The mud splashed around your trousers indicates a lengthy ride in a dog-cart along country roads to a station - for I assume you would not have left your home attired so scruffily - and in your breast pocket I can make out the return half of a Third Class ticket of the Company I have already mentioned, with its characteristic stripe. I cannot, however, at this distance read the destination."

"Really, that is astounding!" Our visitor was speechless and sank onto a chair. "I have but this very day travelled from Headcorn and my congregation is indeed some nine miles distant from that station. Faced with the choice of taking the Kent and East Sussex Railway or a dogcart - well, there was never much doubt, really, despite the mud. But how did you know my - well, my Parish Council was such a source of nervous exhaustion and frustration?"

"Elementary," smiled my friend. "They are ALL such. But what brings you here, may I enquire?"

"Oh sir, Oh Mr. Holmes - I have lost my Faith! Could you help me find my Faith again?"

This was a question that neither I nor Holmes were expecting. Theological speculations and ponderings have never exercised our minds to any great extent, and I confess I know parts of my Bradshaw better than I know parts of my Bible. Both are, in any case, large, heavy tomes that promise to indicate to one where one is heading, information which cannot always be totally relied upon - especially, in my experience, in sections relating either to the Book of Revelation or to the South-Eastern Railway. As though echoing my thoughts Holmes called for the Bradshaw, adding "If we are in luck, we may yet catch what the South-Eastern Line likes to call an "Express Train" and arrive before nightfall."

As we travelled to Charing Cross Station in a hansom our visitor told us a part of his story. It was a tragic tale.

"My name is Reverend Meir Singer. I am not a Christian Minister, but a Cantor, in the Jewish Religion. That is to say, I lead the regular divine services, and sing the Hebrew prayers, and read and chant the Torah from the Holy Scroll. This is what I love to do, and I have done it now in - well, if I recall correctly, in sixteen congregations, from Exeter to North Shields. And at last I could bear it no more. In every synagogue in which I have sung there has been a Committee, or a Board, or a Council, or some such name - the name is not important, for these groups of men are all the same. They all look the same, they all sound the same, they all seem to have similar names and similar twisted personalities. Honestly, if I think back to each of the synagogues where I have sung, I can recall distinctly the pattern on the curtain over the Holy Ark in each one - but the Councils all blur together in my mind and become One Council. They all think they know better than I how to sing, and what to sing, and how to read, and what to read, and what day of the month it is, and what month of the year, and what festival comes next, and who is in hospital, and who needs visiting, and who has an Anniversary to commemorate, and what I am doing wrong, and why I am costing their community too much, and -.... oh, it is a devil's life, I tell you, being Cantor in such synagogues!

And then - just when I was at my most desperate - my Great-Aunt Miriam (May her memory be a blessing!) passed away and left me a small but generous sum of money, which was just what I needed in order to retire. You will understand, Mr. Holmes, that it is very hard to persuade any suitable lady to join a person such as myself in a profession such as mine and so until now I have remained a bachelor. (Not that this has not also been held against me, especially when you realise that every Council contains on average at least three members who have marriageable daughters - or even granddaughters.)

The loneliness of this life was also causing me distress. So, with this small but comfortable sum, I decided upon a Plan. I would retire from this terrible life as a slave to so many congregations, but I would remain what my heart desired - a Cantor. And I would be able at last to marry a lady I have known and admired for some time, Miss Faith Gluckstein of

Stoke-on-Trent. Oh, Faith, my Faith!" - here he blew his nose loudly, clearly overcome by an excess of emotion. "She has also told me that she cannot bear with the situation. She has gone. She has left me. Until, she says, the situation has changed. And it is she whom I wish you to regain and retain for me."

"What situation?" enquired Sherlock, gently, of our overwrought clergyman.

"I will tell you. I searched the Atlas for a town with no Jewish population at all. I hit upon Tenterden in Kent. I went there for a short visit and found an attractive Market Town in pleasant countryside with a mild climate; I discovered for sale a pleasant building with a Hall of suitable size and purchased it. A local joiner soon prepared very passable pews, a reading-desk and Ark, that is the cupboard for the Holy Scroll, and within a few weeks I was able to open my very own Synagogue there.

Oh, Mr. Holmes! I cannot tell you what a joy it was for me. The country air, the fresh country food, and every day I would open up my synagogue (I live in a small flat above it) and sing the Morning Service, loud and clear, just the way I wanted to. Then the day was mine, for there were no crotchety old ladies to visit, no tea to take with frightful wives of dreadful congregants, no sullen Bar-Mitzvah pupils to prepare for hour after hour while their voices prepared to break and ruin all my work - it was idyllic. Around dinner time - earlier in the winter, later in the summer - I would open up again and sing the Afternoon and then the Evening services. Just as I wanted to. My favourite melodies. Repeating sections if I wished.

I stood on the lectern and heard my own voice rolling and echoing amongst the rafters. My Sabbaths were true Sabbaths. My Festivals were Festive. Idyllic, I tell you. And that is how I lived for almost two years. Calm, relaxed, enjoying my religion and my muse. My own synagogue, and not a single other Jew for thirty miles around."

"So what went wrong, and why have you come to us?" asked Sherlock, puffing on his pipe. his brow furrowed. I could tell he was even more puzzled than usual at this strange tale.

"Well, one day - it was just over a year ago - I came one day to the Afternoon Service as usual - and found a man waiting by the door. I asked him what he wanted - I did, after all, get the occasional Commercial Traveller or Wandering Fundamentalist Preacher coming by. It turned out he wished to come to the service - he had made enquiries locally and discovered that my establishment was a synagogue. What could I do? Of course, I let him in.

It was a disaster. He asked me why I sang the "Ashrey" - that is one of our prayers - in a melody different to the one he was used to. He read aloud, in a gabbling voice, while I was trying to compose myself quietly for the next hymn. But I could hardly throw him out, could I? And he came again, and again. It turned out he had taken a lease on a farm near Rolvenden.

A few weeks later another man turned up. A similar tale - he had retired to the country for his health and had taken over a small Grocery establishment in Headcorn. Then another, who was an Agent for a London Brewery, purchasing hops. And within three months I had a small congregation of six, sometimes seven men joining in almost every service. And when I say, "joining in", I mean just that - my privacy had gone.

One day, the first man - Mr. Lewin - asked me who was the President of my congregation. I explained to him, proudly - and now, I realise, foolishly - that there was no such person, that this was my own private synagogue. "That cannot be!" he exclaimed. "Every synagogue needs a President! I shall take this burden upon myself."

In vain I tried to prevail upon him not to undertake this task, to occupy this position. My entreaties fell on deaf ears. By the following Sabbath I was introduced to four of these gentlemen as respectively, now, the President, Vice-President, Honorary Secretary and Honorary Treasurer of the Tenterden Hebrew Congregation. "But there IS no "Tenterden Hebrew Congregation"!" I exclaimed. "There is now," came the response "and I have to tell you, Cantor Singer, that we are not totally pleased with your performance. It is ridiculous that we cannot rely upon a Minyan of worshippers. You are invited to meet with the Board next Tuesday evening."

"A Minyan?" Holmes raised his left eyebrow while enunciating the word, thus making it clear an interrogative was intended. "Yes," explained our new friend, "that is a quorum of ten Jewish men that one technically requires to form a communal Prayer Group. By now there were, as I have said, some six or seven regulars, plus myself, and occasionally another visitor came by, especially during the hop-picking season. But one could not rely on their attendance. And so, at that terrible Board meeting" (he squeezed his eyes shut and shuddered at the memory) "I was told that it was my duty to encourage more "members" to attend services. "But we don't have any members," I said, "I bought this synagogue with my own inheritance."

He paused. "I still recall Mr. Lewin's reply. He said, "We, the Board, have decided on the following Membership Rates. And it is not your place, Cantor Singer, to tell the Board what to do."

His face dropped, and he slumped forward into his seat, sobbing into a grimy handkerchief.

We roused him at Charing Cross and boarded a Dover train, changing at Tonbridge into a "stopper". His face grew visibly greyer as we approached Headcorn. A swift perusal of the Timetable Sheet at that station showed us that no decent train was really due to leave the adjoining Light Railway platform until the following Tuesday - a Market Day - and so we were compelled to hire a conveyance from the landlord of the Station Hotel to take us to Tenterden. I had packed a Gladstone in some haste and Holmes, and I took rooms in a small establishment on the High Street and went to visit the Synagogue.

I confess I have never had much interest in the details of the Hebraic religion but we found - as had been described to us - a small chapel-like room with several rows of pews; towards the front there was a small raised platform with a sloped reading desk, so positioned that the person standing there would be facing a large cupboard over which a crimson cloth with several embroidered symbols was draped. As in all such establishments there was a pervasive odour formed of wax candles, burned wicks and furniture polish. Indeed, I sometimes think that the major difference between the different conflicting denominations is in the smell of the furniture polish they employ. My friend doffed his deerstalker but then, on brief reflection, picked up from a shelf a small black cloth circle, the size of a beermat, and placed it on his head, indicating to me to do likewise.

The sound of voices drew us to a small door near the front; standing near, we could hear a heated conversation taking place in what was apparently some form of vestry. Our new acquaintance was clearly being harangued. "And I tell you, it is of <u>vital</u> importance to the growth of this congregation that we have a valid Mechitza!" came the hectoring voice of a man clearly used to issuing orders.

"And I look to you, as our spiritual leader, to make this point in your next sermon!" A whimper indicated that Cantor Singer was attempting to respond. "And a further point - with whose authority did you travel to London today? This matter was not cleared with the Board. I shall ensure that this matter is discussed fully at the next meeting and the new contract we are preparing to offer you may need to be amended. The synagogue shall not, of course, reimburse your travel costs." With a sweep of his arm Holmes pushed me back as the door opened and two men dressed in dark suits and with bowler hats walked determinedly out and left the chapel, neither looking back nor seeing us. Entering the Vestry, we saw

Singer slumped in a chair, weeping gently. He looked up and saw us, attempted a smile, then buried his nose in a handkerchief. We left him sobbing pathetically and returned to our rooms.

"There is devilish work afoot here, Watson!" My friend spoke for the first time in some two hours, during which he had puffed on his pipe and stared out of the window. "But there is more, much more I need to know. Let us pay another call on our poor friend."

Reverend Singer was at home and offered to make us some tea. I noticed his hand was trembling slightly as he poured the milk. A medical man, of course, is trained to notice such things. "I confess to a certain gap in my comprehension as to the manner in which Jewish communities are organised," said Holmes and, sitting in an armchair, picked up a newspaper lying upon the table. Within minutes he had become so engrossed that his tea grew cold beside him, the biscuits (from a package stamped with primitive Hebraic letters) lay untouched, and I could see that it was not politic to disturb him. So, we left him perusing this and several other similar newspapers and instead I allowed poor Singer to show me his collection of ancient prayer shawls in another room. We were called back to the parlour almost an hour later by a loud exclamation. Hurrying in, I saw Holmes pacing the floor, his eyes gleaming.

"Watson, I have a plan!" he said - a totally unnecessary remark in the circumstances. "We must return to our hotel and make some preparations. Reverend Singer, I understand that Mr. Lewin and the Board have called a meeting with you for the day after tomorrow? Then we have no time to lose. Come, Watson, and thank you for the tea."

Leaving our poor friend bemused, we made our way swiftly to our lodging, where Holmes scribbled a list of items on a sheet of letter paper. Handing it to me, he bade me find the Post Office. "Send a cable to Inspector Lestrade of the Yard - ask him to come down by the next available conveyance and to bring with him the items contained on this list." With this, he sat down, refilled his pipe, and commenced perusing another of the newspapers he had brought back from Singer's rooms.

Lestrade did not arrive until late the following afternoon - he had made the mistake of attempting to travel by the Kent and East Sussex Railway and was in consequence tired and in foul mood from his exertions in assisting to push the little train on its way. But he had brought a suitcase and with a cry of gratitude Holmes took it from him and entered the sleeping quarters, leaving me to explain to the perplexed Inspector the background to our little Kentish adventure. "There is devilish work afoot" was all I could really explain, when the bedroom door opened and a strange and frightful figure emerged.

Logic told me that it could be no other than Sherlock Holmes, but my eyes told me otherwise. Not until the figure spoke could I be reassured by the voice. I barely recognised my friend. He wore a long black wig, curls of hair coiled down besides his ears, his chin was totally concealed by what I assumed to be a beard, if only because there were no legs or tail visible. A black caftan reached almost to his ankles. A dirty white cloth belt dangled from his waist. Most bizarre of all, the caftan parted to reveal that he wore short black knee-length trousers and white leggings!

In all my army career, even in the Khyber Pass, had I rarely seen a figure more bizarre and oriental. But the mischievous ironic smile told me that my friend was more than content with his transformation. It was by now almost evening, and he advised us to partake of some dinner, that he would meet us later.

In fact, although we waited up and tasted several glasses of the local beer, it was not until the following morning that I saw Holmes again; He was tired and indicated that the previous evening had been not only convivial at times but had also included encounters of a less pleasant nature with local ruffians, one of whom had made the grave mistake of pulling at his curled ringlets. I noted that there were still some small bloodstains on his walking stick. Nevertheless, he roused himself towards midday and took lunch with Lestrade and myself. "I believe all is set for tonight's meeting," he informed us. "Lestrade, I would advise you to establish contact with your colleagues in the local Constabulary and advise them to be present in the vicinity. This is a peaceful town but, I suspect, tonight there may well be a Breach of the Peace. Also, I wish you to be on hand to identify me should the need arise." Well, we were of course astonished at this prophecy.

But it was - as I should indeed have known by now, after so many adventures with my friend Sherlock Holmes - a prophecy that was destined to come true. Around the appointed hour of 7 o'clock Lestrade and I made our way to the small Synagogue building, for the meeting of the Board with Reverend Singer was to be held there. On Sherlock's advice Reverend Singer had placed a small notice on the door, stating this to be a "General Meeting of the Tenterden Hebrew Congregation: All Welcome."

Two local Constables greeted us and Lestrade asked them to stand a little distance away, outside a nearby shop. On entering the building, we saw four gentlemen sitting at a long table at the front, two or three others in the pews, and Reverend Singer perched uncomfortably on a small folding chair between them. We were greeted briefly and suspiciously, but it was clear that they did not wish to interrupt the proceedings that had already begun. I was able to understand only a part of what was being said - many technical terms were being bandied, an elderly man in the front pew was wheezing loudly in what I took to be the Yiddish language, and it was clear that the poor Cantor was suffering - when suddenly we heard a strange hullaballoo.

I turned in time to see the door burst open and a band of ragged and rowdy ruffians enter, led by a figure whom I now (thank goodness!) knew to be my good friend and companion in this adventure. The others were strangers but dressed in a variety of dark coats and hats and with unkempt but extensive facial hair. It was clear that they had come to create trouble and - well, I think, dear Reader, that I should be very sparing with my description of the events of the following minutes, for the language and actions employed were most totally unsuited to any occasion in a house of Divine Worship.

Suffice it to say that a mere quarter of an hour later the Constables had cleared the building. On a nod from Lestrade they had released Sherlock and he, with a few words, encouraged them to let the others also go, explaining that he was responsible for their presence. The men received a stern warning and were sent away, with the instruction not to return to Tenterden. Of Lewin and his companions there was no sign. The synagogue showed signs of conflict, with overturned pews, a broken trestle table, papers everywhere, even an upturned inkwell.

Singer, his eyes shining, was straightening the furniture, his hands gripping a bunch of keys. He came to the door to greet us and Holmes advised him to lock the door, go to his rooms to wash and tend to his bruises, and we arranged to meet at our lodgings at the hotel within the hour.

By which time Holmes too had changed to more normal clothing and Lestrade had taken a chair and was looking with some amusement through the small pile of newspapers. We had ordered a simple meal of eggs and fried potatoes and fruit, of which Reverend Singer partook with gusto, clearly in a much better frame of mind than even a few hours previous. I was agitated and wished to learn more about the recent events, which had left me confused and, at times, alarmed. After all, such a brawl as we had witnessed is normally to be experienced only in the lower-class Public Houses at throwing-out time. Holmes poured a generous glass from a bottle of Port, sat back and prepared to answer my eager questioning.

"It was elementary," he explained. "In the fields around Tenterden and Rolvenden at this time of the year are scores, nay hundreds of Hop Pickers - that is to say, Londoners, mainly from the eastern and southern districts of the Metropolis, who come down here to spend a few weeks in the countryside, picking the hops for the breweries and enjoying the fresh country air. Since many come from East London, I made the logical assumption that there would be several of the Hebraic persuasion amongst them. This proved to be correct. From the copies of the "Jewish Chronicle" newspaper which I had read and then borrowed from Reverend Singer it was clear that a theological dispute, indeed several such theological disputes, are raging within the Jewish religion.

All I had to do was to mobilise some of these locally available members of the more fundamentalist wing and use them to oust this self-appointed Board that has been causing such grief to our good friend, the Reverend Singer.

I asked Lestrade here to bring down some items of costume appropriate to the need and went to visit some of the local encampments where the Hop Pickers were enjoying their evening meals. The language barrier was a small problem, as I attempted to adopt an accent indicating not only geographical origins but theological orientations which are, I confess, foreign to me. But, with perseverance, I succeeded. In almost no time at all I had a band of fervent supporters intent on following my every word. This evening I went again and explained that there was a small problem here, and that I required their assistance in the formation of a "Minyan". It was then but a small matter to invade the meeting, seize control of the congregation, and expel the Board."

"But how did you manage it?" asked the Reverend Singer. He was clearly awed by my friend's perspicacity.

"Quite simple," said Holmes, and smiled into his pipe stem. "I simply informed them that Mr. Lewin and his friends were intent on turning the Tenterden Hebrew Congregation into a 'Reformed' Synagogue! The rest - well, the rest just followed naturally. But I would advise you" - he paused to pull briefly on his pipe - "I would advise you to be a little more careful in future as to whom you allow into the services!"

The story almost ends there; The following morning we once again hired a dog-cart to take the three of us - including Lestrade - to Headcorn Station. Reverend Singer waved us off, tears of joy in his eyes; He explained that he had already read the Morning Service and it had been the most spiritual experience for him in several months.

The local joiner was already working on changing the locks on the synagogue doors as we departed. The journey to London was uneventful and I confess I had almost forgotten the entire adventure when, one morning, we received a postcard at 221B Baker Street. It informed us that the Reverend Meir Singer was thankful and proud to announce his impending marriage to a Miss Faith Gluckstein. The ceremony would take place in the Singer Family Private Synagogue, Tenterden, Kent.

My friend smiled and waved the card at me. "You see," he said, "it is indeed possible for a man of the cloth to regain his Faith."

---------------------------------------------

# SQUARING THE CIRCLE

The story I am about to relate comes from the earlier period of my friend's remarkable career, and yet it demonstrates clearly both the excellent reputation he had acquired so early on and the profound effects his intellect has had upon not only the national destinies of our great and other countries, but also upon their industrial development. It was some time in the early 1880's, our good Queen had yet some decades before her and London was expanding at an enormous rate as workers poured in from the surrounding countryside. This had brought with it the need for many more buildings, roads - and other forms of transport.

"This is most strange," said Holmes, laying down the 'Times' and pointing to an item near the bottom of the page. "It appears that a train upon the Underground Railway has vanished. Departed according to its own timetabled path on Tuesday, set off around the Circle, Inner Rail, and has not been seen since."

"Well, it is so dark and smoky down there, I'm not surprised," I said. "Only last week I was making my way through the stygian gloom at Euston Square station, when I lit a match and found myself trying to light my neighbour's cigar. I hadn't even seen he was there."

"Hmmm," responded Holmes, re-reading the item. "That is not quite the same thing. I suspect, however, that our visitor just arriving downstairs might have something to do with the matter."

And indeed, there were sounds of voices downstairs and footsteps approaching the landing. After a brief, perfunctory knock the door opened and a tall gentleman wearing a long dark coat and a broad scarf around his neck entered the room. "Welcome," said Holmes, not getting up. "Take a seat and tell me about your Railway's problems."

Our visitor stood spellbound, opening and shutting his mouth helplessly.

"Well," said Holmes, "I see you are involved in the Underground. Yet not in a criminal capacity, or at least, no more criminal than the normal Railway Director. The Underground is not necessarily the Underworld, though there are times, it is true, that the two are closely allied. You normally travel First Class, and your normal position is on the left side of the compartment, facing the locomotive and the direction of travel. You sometimes travel with the window open."

"But how did you know?" expostulated our visitor.

"It was a matter of mere observation. Your face is blackened, as though by smoke, as is that of most who have to use the Underground Railway. On the left shoulder of your rather dusty coat appears a small burn where a spark from the coal or coke with which, I believe, the locomotives are fired, has clearly landed, indicating that it entered the carriage whilst the locomotive was working hard rather than merely standing at a platform. You would require the scarf to cover your nose and mouth at certain sections where the smoke enters the carriage, when you deliberately leave the window open. Your left elbow shines at a point where you habitually lean upon a carriage window strap, yet when you turned to close the door I noted, if you will pardon my saying so, that the seat of your trousers bears no indication of sitting regularly upon a hard wooden seat such as is provided in the Third Class. Your right shoulder bears a pronounced stoop when you sit before me, indicating that you normally need to hunch it forward and squint at the newspaper you carry, the flickering and inadequate light of the gas lamp being always at the centre of the compartment. So it is clear you are a regular traveller upon the Underground Railway and from the way you entered it is clear you are a person of authority, someone for whom Company's Servants normally open doors, so I deduced you were a Director."

"Sir, I have heard much of you, and what you have just described is the best proof that one can offer that what I have heard is nothing but the truth. In but one detail must I correct you - I am no Director, but Jeremiah Sanderson, the Superintendent of the Line of the Metropolitan Railway Company, and that is why I must sometimes look out of the window to observe as best I can what is happening on our system. I am of course gratified that you have chosen an abode in Baker Street, so close to our own Company's Offices. I come before you with what might appear to be a strange request. But I speak in earnest. We have lost the End of the Line. Since the Inner Circle has been completed by our sister company, the Metropolitan District Railway, forming a continuous loop, our locomotives and trains are enabled to follow the tracks round and round - but we seem to have lost the End. What can we do?

And even worse - our Locomotive Drivers have become so tired of going around in circles, almost constantly in darkness, that they are complaining of Repetitive Train Syndrome and of dizziness caused by constant operation in the same direction. The Outer Rail trains, as you well know, Sir, run clockwise, and the Inner Rail the reverse. In an attempt to banish some of the dizziness and monotony problems, or so they claim, some of the men have taken to traversing the Inner Rail literally anti-clockwise, that is to say, backwards; They depart from Edgware Road at 10am, arrive at Moorgate at Half-Past Nine, and return via Kensington to arrive at Edgware Road almost ninety minutes BEFORE they departed from it. It is causing havoc with our timetables, Sir. Not to mention endless arguments about the men's timesheets."

"An interesting mathematical challenge," observed Holmes. "But do not the passengers complain?"

"Sir, the majority are of course mere Third-Class passengers; Not only do few of them possess a timepiece, but no-one would care to listen to their complaints in any case. Occasionally, it is true, some of the First or Second Class passengers make some comment, but until now we have usually been able to satisfy them with some explanation regarding the different passage of Time underground, away from the sun's rays. But we cannot keep this up for long, Mr. Holmes. We are at our wits' end."

"And this train that disappeared?" asked Holmes, indicating with his long forefinger the news item in the paper.

"Oh that - that was a false alarm, actually. What actually occurred was that the 4.38 a.m. Inner Rail train performed the manoeuvre I have just described, only the driver and fireman were both so confused by the manipulation of Time that they fell into a form of sleepful trance, thinking it was the previous night. The train made three complete circles of the line, not stopping and simply not being seen by any of the station staff as it appeared at a time and place where they were not scheduled to expect a train. Eventually it ended up in a siding near Tower Hill and was found on Wednesday morning. One of the reporters who overheard the Station Master discussing the incident has clearly embroidered the story - but truth to tell, I do not feel we could bear for the truth to be told, for it would make it even harder to attract persons of quality onto our services. As it is, the train in question was used at that hour chiefly by artisans, whom no-one believes in any case. But Mr. Holmes, the entire future of this revolutionary form of transport lies in your hands! We need our Underground Railways! Yet we could be forced to close - and our cities, already choked with traffic, will be strangled by their own development! If we cannot resolve this problem, we shall be ruined! Ruined!" And the poor man sat down, clearly employing great efforts of will to prevent himself weeping.

There was a pause during which Sherlock filled his pipe - he had then but recently taken up this habit - and cogitated. Then, "I think I may be able to assist you in your problems," said Holmes. "I shall require access to the whole line, however, a Timetable and a Pass."

"Of course, Sir! Anything you ask! But what do you intend to do?"

"I do not know yet, my friend. But I am sure that after a pipe or three, some course of action, if not a complete solution, may yet be found. You may leave us now and return to your duties. I shall know where to contact you should need arise."

With expressions of gratitude our dusty neighbour made his way from Mrs. Hudson's lodging house.

"What <u>do</u> you intend to do, Holmes?" I enquired. "First," said he, "We must investigate the sites of these strange incidents. But incognito - I shall not claim the Pass until we have made at least one full circuit of the line, as ordinary passengers."

With this plan in mind we set off without further ado and walked the brief distance to the Underground Railway Station. At this period of which I write it was a mean affair, little more than a shack - the large and magnificent Hotel and Apartment building which stands there now was nothing but a gleam in a Director's eye. Purchasing two tickets to Paddington at the tiny window of the Booking Office, we made our way down the stairs into the stygian gloom below.

Of that journey I can remember but little. I spent a good deal of it crouched near the floor of our compartment, coughing into my handkerchief. But Holmes, I could not help noticing, was puffing vigorously upon his pipe and looking carefully out of the grimy window, opening it at most stations to lean out. "Fascinating," I heard him mutter from time to time, "Fascinating."

When we eventually emerged at Paddington station I felt in dire need of a medicinal brandy and Holmes led me, coughing, to a nearby hostelry. "Drink up, Watson!" he said, pushing a second glass towards me; "For we still have the last part of the Circle to complete!"

"No, Holmes," I said; "I have been a constant friend and companion to you these past years, but I assure you, I shall return to Baker Street by cab. I shall meet you there." And with this I tottered to my feet and went outside to hail a Hansom.

To my astonishment Holmes was already sitting in his normal armchair when I returned to No. 221B. "How did you manage that?" I enquired. "Well, our good friend is correct. When the system is working properly, it does indeed afford expeditious passage beneath the crowded and congested streets," replied Holmes. "The only question is - why does the system not work properly?"

"What is not working?" I asked.

"Oh, so much. So much. Let me recount some of my observations," he said. "Firstly, when I booked our tickets, from Baker Street to Paddington, you will recall, at no point was I asked which way I wished to travel. The clerk assumed - and I can only say logically - that we would go the direct way via Edgware Road. But there was nothing, no sign, not on the pedestrian bridge, not on the platform, to indicate that this was compulsory. So I took us the long way around, via Moorgate and Victoria. Clockwise, on the Outer Rail. I did not want to run the risk of what has been described to us as occurring on the line in the opposite direction - at least, not until I had gained my bearings. On a circular line such as this, it is hard to know what purpose a Return ticket might have, for one can reach one's starting point by continuing forward rather than returning.

The locomotives look smart but unfinished; there are pipes everywhere and the enginemen stand upon their footplates totally unprotected from the smog. In these circumstances it is perhaps unsurprising that they often seek to run backwards, with the chimney and its noisome gases behind them rather than before. I understand from talking to one driver that their engines are called "Bare Peacocks" - why, I can but conjecture; possibly because they lack any form of

43

fantail or board at the rear. The signal lamps are indeed red and green, but so grimy are the glasses - although twice I saw lads wiping them at different stations - that they are barely visible. Speaking of stations, the nameboards are also hard to read in the smoky gloom and were it not for the porters calling out whatever it is porters do call out (for I confess it is often hard to distinguish human cries from the animal grunts they make) there would be almost no chance of learning when one had arrived at one's destination - and were this to have been missed, the only alternative would normally be to make yet a further circuit of the line. Yes, there is much here, I see, that needs consideration. I will call you, Watson."

And so saying he sat himself deeply down in the chair and closed his eyes in meditation.

It was but three days later that he sent one of his 'Baker Street Runners' to me, a grubby urchin bearing a note stating that he would be gratified were I to present myself at four o'clock. At the appointed hour I attended as requested and found Sherlock looking tired, with grime on his face making it hard to distinguish the grey rings around his eyes.

He was hunched over a large foldable map of London and on the floor and his reading table were a variety of timetable folders, several past volumes of Bradshaw and a copy of a journal which he showed me with some humour in his tired eyes - "The Railway Magazine."

Before he had a chance to tell me anything, the bell rang again and soon Mrs. Hudson was presenting our earlier visitor to us once more. He looked, I could not help noticing, even more wan under the grime that covered his features. But he brightened up when, divested of coat and top hat and scarf, he was invited to take a seat next to the fire.

Following a cup of tea Sherlock sat back and commenced his explanation. "It has been, for me, a fascinating few days," he began. "I began with a further two complete circuits of the Circle Line, in each direction, alighting at certain stations en route to test the atmosphere. I also travelled upon a couple of the branch lines which diverge from the so-called Circle. It is, of course, actually more of a misshapen Oval, but since the Oval has been taken as a station name by a competing Railway, I can understand why the term is avoided. It is indeed an intriguing place to travel and to work. One could almost be in Hades rather than Hammersmith. The line first opened only in 1863, I gather, and yet the amount of soot clinging to all parts of the tunnels makes it a veritable sweep's paradise. The blackness of the hole matches the blackness of the soul - my apologies, by the way, Mr. Sanderson, I trust you do not take offence."

Sanderson nodded. "Fear not, Mr. Holmes, I have served my time with the Company for over fourteen years now, and there is rarely a day when my wife does not cry with rage at the dirt engrained in every orifice of my clothing. Day and night, I am on duty. Sometimes there have been weeks when I have not seen the sun, even in the open cuttings, due to the thickness of the smoke; and it is hardly surprising that my dear wife bore only two years ago a child, our fifth, who is himself totally black."

Holmes sat back, a curious expression on his features. "Ah yes. I understand, Mr. Sanderson, that you reside near Aldersgate Station, not very far from the Docks?"

"That is the case, Mr. Holmes. I need to be within easy reach of the Line at any time."

"Quite so."

Holmes turned once more to his notebook. "At first it was hard to decide where to start. This is the concomitant of your own problem, is it not, of not knowing where to end? But then I had a stroke of good fortune.

I discovered what amounts almost to a secret society of persons who name themselves "Railwayacs." Persons - mostly of respectable age and circumstances, it seemed, several are even of the Cloth - who devote their leisure hours to the pursuit of locomotives, who haunt obscure corners of obscure stations, who sit in the carriages with a note pad on their knee and mark with a pencil the exact stopping time at each station or indeed, leaning into the smoke, recording the point at which a certain milepost is passed. I first became aware of this phenomenon when travelling in a compartment on a clockwise train, leaning out of the window in an effort (vain, as it turned out) to see which station we had just passed, when a gentleman leaning out of the other window turned to me and called out "Did you get it?" I confess I was for a moment alarmed and was glad to have my trusty knobkerry with me but it transpired, as the conversation developed, that he had been referring to the number of the locomotive hauling the Anti-Clockwise train which had just passed us. Since I had also been leaning out, he had assumed I was searching for this information, trying to 'spot' the number.

For some reason these persons gain what appears to be an inordinate amount of pleasure from writing lists of numbers and then underlining or striking through each one when it represents a locomotive they have" - he looked down at his notepad - "er, 'copped.'

Furthermore, there are sections and sub-sections of the Railwayac Fraternity. This first acquaintance introduced me at Kings Cross station to three other members of the sect and it was from them that I learned of the existence of this journal, which I purchased later at the bookstall.

Others gathered around us, wielding a variety of notebooks and patent binoculars. But one was, it seems, a collector of used tickets, whereas another perused timetables in order to analyse the possible speeds to be attained by the express trains of several of the major Companies. Yet another was able to tell me - though I had not asked - the exact length of each siding along the Great Northern Railway, both Down and Up sides, between Kings Cross and Huntingdon. It was," he paused, reflectively, "a lengthy performance, I confess. I, who have observed so much of the world, discovered a whole new dimension to the landscape around me, a landscape filled normally with smoking locomotives and steaming, screeching carriages. But it struck me that perhaps these fanatics could supply me with some missing details, some insights into the inner workings of the Railway mentality. And so it proved."

We leaned forward, expectantly, but alas, Sherlock chose this moment to knock out his pipe and commence filling it once more with fresh tobacco. We waited, elated but frustrated.

"Yesterday evening I attended a meeting of these gentlemen. The meeting was advertised in this Magazine and took place in an obscure Church Hall in a rather poorer part of London - I shall not bore you with the details. Some twenty middle-aged and, as I say, relatively respectable gentlemen had gathered to attend a lecture, indeed a learned discourse, upon the latest developments on the Midland Railway, accompanied by lantern slides. The lecture was accompanied by various remarks and followed by a quite heated discussion on such matters as 'bogies' and 'singles' and 'superheating' and 'double-heading' and other terms of which I understood but little. I thought at first that 'double-heading' meant being in two minds about something, but most of these Railwayacs seem to be, if anything, single-minded. Or maybe even less than that.

At first I was left out of the discussion but - well, you know me, Watson - I was soon able to bluff my way into the debate with a few enquiries which indicated that I was by no means expert and yet, at the same time, not wholly uninformed. Following the termination of the meeting there were copious amounts of the refreshing beverage and an opportunity for less strenuous conversation. Each person appeared to be a specialist in something quite different and yet they shared enough in common to be able to converse in comradely manner with each other.

I mentioned my interest in the history and operations of the Metropolitan Railway and was slightly surprised to be treated with scorn. "Oh that? That's just a clockwork circle," said one; "It's all in tunnel, can't see a blasted thing," said

47

another. "I hear people go out of their minds in the dark," said a third. "Give me a clear mainline in the open air," said another; "Then a man can see what's in front of him and around him." The others appeared in agreement.

Pursuing the matter a little - for I was already aware that at least <u>some</u> of these Railwayacs had an interest in subterranean means of locomotion - I learned that those who devoted themselves to Underground systems were looked upon as a form of sub-species, a *rara avis*, not quite up to the standard of the man who could list each lever in a signal box in the Scottish Lowlands. "It's the lack of oxygen" said one, more scientifically. "There's not enough to breathe down there, everyone knows that; You can cope for a journey or two, but then you need to get out into the fresh air. Otherwise it'll affect your mind."

I thanked the gentlemen and took my departure. Returning - by the Metropolitan, of course - I took the liberty of approaching the engine driver upon his locomotive. He jumped at first, not having seen me coming along the platform and being suspicious of my motives - "Ye're not goin' to cab MY injin!" he roared initially. He softened slightly when I showed him my Pass and explained I was undertaking a commission for the Superintendent of the Line. How long, I asked him, did he work each day on these trains?

He required some thought and time to answer, it was clear he did not possess enough fingers, and I nearly missed the reply as the Guard's whistle shrilled out of the gloom, but he answered "Fourteen hours" as he pulled whatever lever he needed to pull to get his train once more under way.

And so, Mr. Sanderson, I would put to you what I have learned. The drivers, stokers and other persons in your Company's employ clearly work long hours - as, I need hardly add, do you yourself. Yet even amateur experts in railway operation claim that excessive exposure to the smog in your Company's tunnels can lead to a miasmic influence upon the human intellect. I must presume, despite - I might add - some evidence to the contrary, that your Company's staff are human, and not demonic imps, though when seen by gaslight against the red of the open firebox and the black of the swirling smoke, with long-handled shovels in their hand, I did get a rather luciferian impression.

The consequence is that they, as you so eloquently put it to us earlier, have lost the End of the Line. Their circular motions create a form of 'perpetuum mobile' which unhinges their internal orientation - always so important in any case when travelling in the dark - a disorientation made in this case worse by the constant circular forward motion, compounded by the rattling and shaking of the locomotives and the inhalation of the gaseous fumes.

I can make only two possible recommendations," added Holmes, gravely. "Either your Directors must permit the men to work shorter hours - something which, I fully realise, is more than unlikely. Or, they must create a system which offers the drivers and others some alternative to the continuous circular and subterranean progress. Somewhere where the Drivers, Stokers, Guards and others can get occasional opportunities to enjoy fresher air, more light, some exposure to the external elements, and where they can traverse a route which has both a Beginning and an End, thus also contributing to their mental equilibrium. And if you organise this correctly," he added, "your Directors may even be able to obtain some lucrative property and traffic possibilities, whilst at the same time improving the health of their Company Servants. All of which would redound to your credit."

As a result of this advice, over the next few years the Metropolitan constructed a railway from Baker Street Station out through Hampstead and Harrow and to Uxbridge but mainly on to Amersham and into the wilds of the Chilterns, eventually to a halt in the middle of a field, which they named Quainton Road as no village or even hamlet was nearby. Thence, through acquisition, they added a further twig off the branch, to a field near the mere village of Brill. Here was truly a place deserving of the title "End of the Line." Another extension was constructed to a nowhere sort of place where the Metropolitan converged with the cross-country branch-line of the Nor'Western, a place which was named Verney Junction in honour of Vernon and Rodney Spence, the sons of one of the senior drivers, Siamese twins who were inextricably joined and yet maintained they found pleasure from watching trains pass the Incurables Home near Harrow.

The Engine Drivers and Guards would be sent upon their duties at least once each six working days into this fresh air and sunlight, and this enabled them to maintain their biological rhythms and health to a far greater extent than heretofore. This was maintained until - though I glance ahead somewhat - the tunnel and some other sections had been electrified, thus removing the need for the further reaches of these extensions, which were then eventually disposed of and closed.

And as a reward Holmes was presented by the grateful Directors with a Free Lifetime Pass upon all lines and trains of the said Metropolitan Railway.

As he observed to me at the time, a rare smile suffusing his normally severe aquiline features as he showed me the fine gold engraved disc attached to its leather strap, "See, a Complimentary, my dear Watson".

................................................

## THE CASE OF THE HORN IN THE FOG

"Confound this fog!" I confess I was quite annoyed. I was suffering still from some slight breathlessness and the effects of a tremendous blow to my head from a stick wielded by a burly ruffian. My friend Sherlock Holmes smiled to himself and sat back in his leather armchair, filling his pipe. It was still only early evening, yet the view outside was totally invisible. "Tell me again, my friend, exactly what happened," he said.

"Well, as I have said, I was walking here, as usual. I had taken the Metropolitan Railway train and had got out at Baker Street Station as usual; the eastbound platform. There was hardly any difference between the atmosphere in the tunnel and that outside the station. The fog of course was appalling, and I may have stopped to cough a little. Be that as it may, I entered what, I assure you, I considered to be the door to these very lodgings, Holmes. Indeed, so sure was I, that I never looked up as I climbed the stairs and took off my coat and hat before entering - well, before entering what I thought was this room. I tell you; I was utterly taken aback by what I saw."

"Do tell me again," said Holmes, leaning forward, his keen eyes blazing beneath his brown eyebrows.

"Well, there were ladies – well, women - girls - females, several of them, at least five. They were sitting in armchairs. Ghastly things, pink and purple. Stuffed and straining at the seams. The chairs, I mean. The wallpaper was pale green. There was a fire burning and it was very warm in the room. In fact, I felt suddenly very hot - especially after the change from the climate outside this wretched establishment. I began to perspire.

The ladies - women - girls - were wearing, were wearing...... well, actually, they appeared to be wearing very little. Very little indeed. Corsets, and flimsies, and that sort of

51

stuff. I'm dashed if I know what the wretched things are called. It's all - well, female stuff. But I tell you, it was most disconcerting!"

"And so?" asked my friend. It was annoying. I had already told the story once, but he was clearly intrigued and wished to hear it again. "And so I turned round and went down the stairs. Clearly, I had entered 221A, or 221, or 119 Baker Street, by mistake. And this is what I told the ruffian who appeared at the bottom of the staircase. But he didn't seem to believe me."

"Now tell me please once more, exactly what he said," said Holmes, closing his eyes and leaning backwards. "Maybe we can get to the bottom of this most upsetting act of unprovoked violence."

"I said, first, politely, that I wished to pass. He made no reply but just grunted and stood in my way at the bottom of the stairs. I repeated my desire to leave and he asked, "What did you come for?" I said, "I must have made a mistake, I could not see, I groped and came because of the fog." Then he said - it was a strange accent, I'll allow you, maybe Irish - "And did you enjoy de grope and de fog?" Well, I ask you, what a strange question!"

"Yes, most strange," repeated Holmes. His voice seemed distant.

"Well, of course I responded, "No, I did NOT enjoy the fog, and that is why I must leave here and go to the place I first intended." To which HE said, "Not without paying, squire." "Pay for what?" I remonstrated, fearing an act of thievery. His answer, so far as I recall, went: "You come in, you go up, you take coat off, you come down, you horny, you pay for de fog!"

"And then?"

"There appears to be some misunderstanding," I said. "I am an Englishman, I have no horn and I do NOT pay for fog!" At which point - well, I was putting my arm in my jacket and was at a disadvantage - he hit me over the head with a stick. I must have been momentarily stunned, for when I came to - my wallet was gone. What could I do? I had no wish to ascend those stairs again. The hall was dark and empty. I decided to come round here and eventually managed to recognise the correct door. And my head still hurts damnably."

Holmes laughed. I was rather angered by this.

"It appears, my old friend," he said, "that you have been the victim of several misunderstandings at the same time. Naturally I am distressed at your contusions and your financial loss and we shall send a message round to Lestrade at the Yard immediately, so that those concerned may be apprehended. I have no doubt the wallet may be recovered, and possibly even some of its contents. But I am intrigued as to the nature of the establishment upon which you stumbled and also its apparent proximity to these humble lodgings - for, in the many years I have been privileged to pay my monthly contribution to support Mrs. Hudson's widow's pension, not once have I heard sounds of gaiety issuing forth from neighbouring windows, nor encountered the denizens of this pit of iniquity upon the local streets. Clearly this is something which demands - and soon - some closer investigation. In view of the proximity of the "*mise en scène*", so to say, I shall have to take to an appropriate disguise. Watson, I beg you, do go carefully in this fog but leave now. If you would be so kind as to return this time tomorrow, I may have some more news for you."

Nursing my bruise, I had little option but to comply with this request.

The next day which, fortunately, was a little clearer, I repaired once more to my friend's apartments. He was enjoying a cup of brandy by the fire as I entered and seemed, I was heartened to see, in jovial mood. Without much ado he poured me also a generous tumbler and commenced his tale.

"It was clear to me that your unfortunate experiences of yesterday must have been the result of a typical misunderstanding, exacerbated perhaps by linguistic infelicities. Once you had gone I attired myself in a suitable costume - though I shall not describe it to you, my old friend, if you do not mind - and set off for Baker Street Station, determined to follow your trail. I had some clues to guide me from your account, plus you had - I regret to say - clearly trodden in at least two different mounds of canine deposit, one on each shoe, and one equine deposit, on your left shoe. Don't worry, old chap, Mrs. Hudson is very good with brush and shovel. But from these deposits I deduced that you had walked through the Hackney Carriage rank outside the station, keeping this to your left.

The deposits were, may I say, still relatively fresh and demonstrated a horse that had been well-fed and well-cared for; there was no street mud mixed with it. Using this as a starting point I headed from the station and soon encountered, on the right side of the pavement, the remains of what you had quite clearly stepped into with your right foot. The pile into which your left foot had stumbled in that fog took me, I confess, somewhat longer to track down, and also brought me into some unfortunate conversations with street urchins and others as I attempted, stooping, to compare the crumbling fragments I had extracted from our stair carpet with various offerings left by, shall I say, over-generous canines. There was, I might add, an over-abundance of possible clues. But eventually I found the house entrance which most likely simulated that described by you - that is to say, looking - even in the daylight - remarkably like our very own.

I applied for entrance and found that the door opened swiftly, and I was beckoned inside. The man inside - indeed, of ruffianly appearance - indicated that I should ascend the staircase to the upper floor, from whence could be heard the sound of female voices engaged in light-hearted conversation; but I advised him that I had other desires and, were he not to co-operate, he would feel the end of my knobkerry. Strangely, this remark did not have the initially-desired effect - for of course, I had neglected to bear in mind that a secret of any successful business is to employ staff who would not, themselves, be tempted by the merchandise on sale. But after some delicate, ah, negotiations, a satisfactory conclusion was, er, reached, and indeed I am more than happy, dear friend, to present you now with your wallet. You should find that the contents include all that you lost, plus a small additional sum for inconvenience and distress. And a small ticket which, you will note, permits you one visit to the establishment - the correct address is on the reverse side - entirely free and without cost, as a further form of compensation.'"

    I was aghast. "What, Holmes!" I cried.
    "Yes," he smiled. "A Complimentary, my dear Watson."

………………………………….

# THE CASE OF THE FINAL CURTAIN

"Aha!" My friend Sherlock was excited. I could tell the signs, the quavering joy in his voice, the way his left hand shook as he held the late-night edition of 'The Times' raised before him. "Aha again!" he added, perhaps a little less necessarily this time as he had already gained my attention, disturbing my own quiet perusal of a rather interesting and well-illustrated volume of anatomic studies of the female form, which I had of course purchased purely for the sake of my further medical education. I always maintain that one can never know enough about such things, even if, like me, one is not actually specialising in Gynaecology.

"Well, Holmes?" I enquired in as friendly and curious a voice as I could muster at the time – I would be prepared to swear I had never known that – but no, let me concentrate on the case I am about to describe.

"Well indeed!" he responded. "What an amazing matter, eh? Amazing, truly amazing, don't you think?"

"I say, Sherlock," I protested. "I really have no idea what you are talking about."

"Last night. Watson, last night at the Strand. The Strand Theatre I mean. A murder! A veritable murder! On the stage, in full public view – but a real one, Watson on the stage but not a stage murder, and no-one Watson, NO-ONE can claim to have seen the murderer! What about that, eh? And I wonder, by the way, whether the person who has just rung our bell so determinedly, even viciously, may or may not have something to do with the matter!"

Indeed, there was some commotion downstairs and then the sound of heavy boots ascending the steep staircase. The door was then not just opened but swung open, melodramatically, and a man stood in the open doorway – a cape over his shoulders, a top hat in his left hand.

"Please enter," said Holmes, "Or, if you prefer, please make an entrance. For a left-handed thespian of some years' successful theatrical career, happily married and yet with a slight snuff problem, you have nothing to fear of us. Please take a seat. You need not bestride this humble room like a stage."

Our visitor gaped. So often have I witnessed this reaction to my friend's lightning-quick assessment of some stranger, purely from their external and unconscious signs. "I, I..." he stammered but Holmes smiled gently, even patronisingly, and with a gesture of his hand waved him to silence.

"I am sure that it is unusual for an actor of your experience to stammer or be speechless," he began. "But really, it is obvious. You stand there like someone accustomed to applause at their entrance; you appear well-nourished and you wear a clean collar – not something universal amongst those of the acting profession, or so I understand, especially those forced to reside in theatrical lodgings. So clearly there is someone caring for you, even if you return home only late each evening. As for the snuff – well, look at your right sleeve, which indicates that you normally use your left hand to apply the substance to your nostrils. Now, what can we do for you? I trust this is something to do with the unfortunate events at the Strand Theatre?"

"By Jingo, Mr. Holmes, but it really is true, what they say about you, eh?"

"Well, I do hope not quite <u>all</u> of what they say about me...." murmured Holmes, flushing slightly. "But a great deal, yes, I do believe so. Now, what is the problem?"

"Well, in this case, the poor man never got his Curtains."

"I believe it is considered a bad thing for an actor to die on the stage?" asked Holmes.

"Well, it depends what you mean. I am, although I have not yet had the chance to introduce myself properly, Josiah

Greenhalgh, Manager of the Strand Theatre these past three years. It is not an easy life, Mr. Holmes, coping with the vagaries of playwrights and directors, of casts and orchestras, of stage staff and the petty-minded, smutty-minded censors of the Lord Chancellor's Office. Before I took this post I was Superintendent of a Home for Nervous Cripples near Eastbourne and after the sudden and early demise of my predecessor, due to a heart attack in the middle of the Season, I was approached by some of the Directors of the Strand Theatre, who knew of me since they had sent several of their players to our care over the years, and they asked if I would take upon myself the responsibility for this position. It was considered that I already possessed most of the requisite qualities, even though I had had no experience of the professional theatre world. But I have learned, Mr. Holmes, I have learned fast. I have had to.

The actors and actresses all love a really drawn-out Death scene. But they want the public to react, to respond, to empathise with them as they appear to die. I think you are referring to something different when you mention 'Dying on stage', if I may say so, and that is the term when an actor says a line and the audience simply fails to appreciate it, they neglect to laugh when they should or to weep when they should. All actors wish to be loved, Mr. Holmes. That is what drives them. And it is because so many of them are, I must admit, rather unsuccessful in this matter in ordinary life, that they grow up wishing to portray, for a few hours at least, somebody else, a totally different character, one who may attract the sympathies of the public in a way that they themselves fail to do in their normal daily lives.

It is an understanding, Mr. Holmes, an unspoken understanding. Deep down they know that the public come merely to be entertained and are prepared indeed to pay for this privilege, and that they earn their meagre wages only by pretending to be someone else than whom they really are. But you can perhaps understand how easy it is in such circumstances to become, shall we say, slightly unhinged? To lose touch with reality. Completely and utterly."

"You are, I see, a philosopher of some depth too. I am impressed," said Sherlock, and I was myself somewhat astounded, for it was very rarely indeed that my good friend, of whom Modesty could not be claimed to be one of his faults, should make such an utterance. "May it be possible perhaps for my friend and I" – here he nodded in my direction – "that we could perhaps take up some minor role in your current production and so gain opportunity to see your House from within?"

"But of course, Mr. Holmes!" replied our visitor. "I should be more than pleased to arrange that. Of course, I should need to provide Equity cards for you."

"That would be most equitable," responded Holmes. "Naturally we would be more than satisfied with only minor roles, as Extras, I believe they are called, but they should be walk-on parts so that I can also observe the arrangements of the stage, as well as behind the stage, without attracting any attention from this murderer who is clearly so keen to remain unknown."

That same afternoon we were met at the Stage Door – where I used to wait so often in my own younger student days, in the often forlorn hope of enticing one of the young exquisite things to partake of some supper with me – and were shown briefly around the establishment. It had been decided to continue the run of the current production "A Quite Normal Scoundrel", using the Stand-In Henry Jeveson to replace the previous night's murder victim, Arnold Stult.

Indeed, tongues wagging around us behind the stage suggested that this was a deliberate ploy by the management, for the House had been falling significantly in the past three days and yet tonight a full sell-out of all available tickets had been expected.

59

And this indeed proved to be the case. The theatre was literally packed, mainly, I gathered, not with seasoned devotees of drama but with those hoping for a further concrete demonstration of human mortality. Our task, Holmes and mine, was to stand, suitably costumed and with besmeared visages, as members of a crowd at Stage Centre Left during Act One Scene Four and then again to be moving around in an agitated and angry crowd scene from Stage Left to Right and partway back again during Act Three Scene Six – the ultimate scene and for Holmes doubly important, because it was at this climactic point that not one shot (as in the script) but two had rung out, and not only had the main character and villain of the piece, Sir Jasper Golightly, as played by Arnold Stutt, dropped to the ground but he had done so indeed more lifelessly than the stage directions (and union regulations) had demanded, leaving indeed a smear of blood that had not been wholly washed away by the housekeepers. Our instructions had been simple – "Just do what the rest of the extras in the crowd are doing" – and our positions as anonymous seekers of the truth meant that we could hang around backstage, chat flirtatiously with some of the younger actresses, prowl around on the pretext of looking for the lavatories (though later on I wished fervently that we had never found them) and generally get in the way of the stage hands with their ropes and rolled canvases and pieces of furniture. Just like everyone else, in fact.

Holmes had considered from the outset that it had to have been an 'inside job' somehow, carried out at the very least by someone who knew the script totally and could tell almost to the second when a shot was due to be fired at the chief villain, and so employing this opportunity to fire a live rather than a blank charge.

So, he played close attention to various persons employed, or looking as though they were probably paid to be employed, even though they seemed idle and motionless, in various positions around the theatre. (There are many such in the theatrical profession for the Union regulations demand that persons be paid for a whole evening even if they only have two lines to say at the end or commence the production playing a corpse on the stage at the very beginning of the piece; Since Writers do not have a Union they are still only paid by the line, whereas Actors and Technicians are paid by the evening.) Which of them would have had an opportunity to pull a revolver at the vital moment, unseen, to take aim and squeeze the trigger? In the general hubbub and commotion of the previous evening no-one had thought to search the building straight away or to take a roll-call.

Holmes used his spare moments from our undemanding thespian responsibilities to chat in a casual fashion with the other actors, employing a variety of working-class accents. "So this Arnie, a bit of a nob were 'e, then?" I overheard at one point, and "Tut, shocking, what modern hacteresses have come to" on another occasion. As we were having our facial make-up corrected and refreshed before the final scene, he chatted with the make-up artistes, giving the impression generally of a garrulous bore who could not refrain from idle chit-chat. This of course, lowered the defences of some of the other cast members, all of whom were still under some shock from the events of the previous performance.

The plot of this melodrama was not particularly demanding. There was a Maiden and she had her Lover who loved her - but only from afar - for her purity and her daintiness, but there was also a Villain who had Designs upon said Maiden, the main design being that she should cease to be a Maiden at all and become instead just one of his Cast-Offs within the Cast.

Even standing on the stage in the crowd scenes it was fairly tedious and predictable, so what it was like for the paying public one shudders to think. But at the final scene comes the climax, where the hero Jack (played by Ernest Mason) confronts the Villain Sir Jasper (oh, how unoriginal these tinpot playwrights are) at the market place and a fatal shot is fired – although, just to make it quite clear who is the Hero, it is the Villain who pulls the revolver on the Hero, the Hero grapples with him, the Villain fights back, a shot rings out – and, as one can guess, the Villain falls. Technically he is meant to say as he falls "You are right, Jack, I am not worthy of her" and it was the failure of this parting line as much as the second shot that had indicated to the rest of the cast that something untoward had occurred. No actor likes to miss his final line. However, since Arnold Stutt, playing Sir Jasper Golightly, had twisted in several directions during this final brief wrestling, it had proved impossible even for Scotland Yard's finest ballistic experts to ascertain from which direction the fatal live second shot had been fired.

Well, the performance reached its – for want of a better word – climax and Henry Jeveson pulled his revolver, Ernest Mason playing Jack grappled with him, they twisted to and fro and then at last from off-stage a loud report was heard, Henry fell, said, "You are right, Jack, I am not worthy of her" and promptly and theatrically expired. At which point the audience booed! Before the curtain could even come down, and starting in the upper circle, those who had paid to come and see "a real murder" booed their dissatisfaction out! The curtain fell, the actors rose or relaxed to their normal positions and left the stage, grim-faced. There would be no curtain calls that evening.

The next morning the 'Morning Post' had a quite amusing little feuilleton on the matter – on the lack of decent murders in modern British Drama, "Where are the MacBeths of our day?" and so forth. The 'Times' of course was more restrained, as one would expect, merely pointing out that times should have moved on since audiences flocked to the stadia to observe how gladiators cut each other into pieces.

Holmes and I were tired, for there had been a lengthy discussion following the close of the performance the previous evening with several of the principal actors expressing their deep dissatisfaction with the management and even the voiceless Extras voicing their displeasure, for they had been denied their chance to appear once more and bow in a row at least once as the curtain rose and fell.

Eventually most of the cast and some of the stage hands (even though they belonged to a different union and were much better paid) had adjourned to the nearby 'Scene-Shifter's Arms' to consume more than a little alcoholic refreshment and to assuage their injured feelings also with whelks, mussels, jellied eel and other disgusting fare. (As a medical man I am often alarmed by the food provided in public houses; Possibly the purveyors are relying upon the purchasers being too much under the influence of alcohol as to wonder where the various molluscs served may have originated – from the mudflats below the sewage outfall pipes into the Thames. I swear, should anyone ever fall upon the idea of slicing a cheap and humble potato very thinly and deep-frying it, scattering thereupon some obnoxious chemical flavour such as onions combined with cheese or even salt mixed with vinegar, he could probably make a fortune by selling them in little over-priced bags in these establishments – people need something to nibble upon to accentuate their thirst while drowning the flavour of the beer, they desire something wholly unhealthy and non-nutritious, something they would only purchase if already slightly under alcoholic influence. But I digress, and maybe this is an idea ahead of its time.)

In any case, Sherlock and I were there to keep our ears open for any hint that might assist us in tracking down the murderer, any personal conflicts within the cast. And good heavens, there were so many! By about midnight it seemed that we had each of us individually heard almost every member of the cast complaining bitterly and emotionally about each other member of the cast as well as the Director, the Company's Manager, the Theatre Manager and the designer of the posters, who had without fail, it seems, used too small a type-face for their names and placed them in the wrong position, too far down. Not to mention the author, who had not given them enough lines, or the wrong ones. After a while the sameness of these complaints began to become apparent and we made our way back to our rooms, where Sherlock then spent at least two hours in making notes, trying to recall as accurately as possible what each of his interlocutors had expressed. So it was in the small hours when he turned down the gas lamps and retired.

The next evening, in view of the lack of results for our client, we felt we had little option but to resume our temporary thespian careers and observe and listen further. This time the house was only half-full; all went according to its wonted routine, Sir Jasper rose from the dead in order to take his curtain calls – only two really, as it turned out, for by the third rising of the curtain half of the audience had already donned capes and hats and had begin to make their way to the evening drizzle outside.

But Sherlock had spent a goodly part of the evening chatting idly backstage with Griselda LaBelle, the actress who played the maiden Mary, and when the rest of the cast left at the end to remove to the 'Scene-Shifter's Arms' he came over to me and said, "Be a good chap, will you, keep your eyes and ears open, make what notes you can, discreetly, and I shall pursue this particular line of enquiry in a quieter place. I will see you back at Baker Street." I had little option but to obey as he escorted Griselda to a Hansom cab and they drove off, the wheels splashing through the puddles of the Strand.

I did as I had been commanded, for as an old Army man one knows the value of obedience and of good Intelligence in the field. I returned alone to our Rooms at 221B Baker Street and awoke alone and breakfasted alone too on Mrs. Hudson's poached eggs, of which Holmes had once said, they were good evidence that sometimes poachers made the best gamekeepers. It was not until shortly before lunchtime that my friend returned home, pale and tired with grey bags beneath his eyes.

Over a cup of tea he spoke to me of his experiences of the previous night. "Griselda LaBelle is of course her stage name, Watson," he began, stirring his cup and then adding just a dash of brandy to it from the decanter upon the mantlepiece. "Her given name, at the font, is Mabel Longbottom. She was born in Fleetwood, a town better known for fishing fleets than for acting. From the 'Mabel' she took the 'LaBelle' as a surname. As for the 'Longbottom' – well, she does indeed have one that could be so described. I confess it did not take me long to inveigle myself into her trust, Watson. Even Sir Jasper could have taken lessons from me, and to his profit.

After a chop or two and some red wine at Simpsons further along the Strand and then some champagne (though not of the best and most expensive quality, I could not bring myself to waste such upon her, so I stuck to the '82 Moët) it did not take long for me to hear all her secrets, even those – especially those – that I did not really wish to hear." He shuddered slightly, his eyes closed, his face drawn.

"I will spare you the details, my friend, but suffice it to say that her boudoir looked as though several cats had been needlessly slaughtered in it, for all is pink or red or covered in fur. I had already gathered that she is somewhat unpopular amongst many of the cast – they call her 'The Witch' because she keeps speaking of needing a new broom.

By this I mean that she has already insisted to the management upon the replacement of no fewer than three former actors who had played the role of Sir Jasper Golightly.

She makes her demand very loud and very public, she says "I refuse to play any more against this man!" - she accuses them of making eyes at her during the more intimate scenes, and so forth. In vain do the actors in question complain that this is all a part of their role and that they have no real interest in her apart from a purely professional one – this only enrages her even the more.

The management always caves in to her demands, for she is the only person in the Company considered worthy of letters of the size and flourish and colour upon the posters as to attract a reasonable number of 'punters', as they are called, who would then be likely to part with their shillings and sixpences. Three actors have left the company in humiliation and rage, Watson, in this season alone, and the late Arnold Stutt would have been the fourth. But he refused to go! He claimed he had a contract for three months and he would play the role or die in the attempt! Brave but, as it turned out, foolish words, Watson, typical of the bravado of the type of character actor who can play such a dastardly villain so well. This I heard from our Mr. Greenhalgh.

So after some considerable exertion – physical as well as intellectual - I finally got this vexatious damsel to confess to me what she had done. I find, Watson, that on occasion a head on a pillow will reveal much, much more than over a table in an interrogation room at the Yard. She took me, of course, to be a fellow actor, one who would understand and sympathise with her views, since I still had costume and make-up on as we left the theatre last night. Within ninety minutes, Watson, both were off, yet she considered informing me that she would not take it amiss were I to apply for the role of Sir Jasper myself, should anything amiss ever happen to Henry Jeveson.

"What could go amiss, Miss?" I asked, innocently, and she laughed in what was meant to be a pretty way and said, "Well, maybe he might break not just a leg but his neck too."

As you will know, Watson, to say "Break a leg" is considered amongst members of the acting profession to be almost a greeting, a good wish, a term of endearment.

So when I asked again, following some further exertions, why this should be, and once she had calmed down and got her breath back, she said, "Why, it is up to me to judge who could be a good enough villain as to seduce the young Mary. Ronald Atherthorpe was not interested in women at all,

Mark Morris was impotent, Derek Flynn is singularly under-endowed. Arnie Stutt came to me here once but then had the gall, the temerity to say he did not wish to come to my boudoir again! So he had to go. Henry Jeveson – well, he is a bit of a cold fish. But you, my dear, you fulfil all that I seek in a villain!"

    I presume, Watson, she meant this as a compliment, but it was at the same time clear to me now who had committed the murder and Why. The When and the Where we knew, of course. It only remained to find out How. And this information she also volunteered, after some further glasses of cheap red wine.

    You will recall, Watson, that when you and I and maybe some eighteen other Extras are thronging the stage in that final scene, the character Mary is placed behind us at the window of her cottage, threatening to leave for Australia and there regain what she can of her honour. Then the fight scene takes place and all eyes are naturally upon the combatants and Mary is shielded from sight in any case in this cardboard cottage to Stage Left.

    So it was from there, Watson, unseen by any hands behind the stage or eyes in the audience, that she took her deadly aim and ended Arnold Stutt's theatrical career so dramatically and then concealed the weapon in the frilly décolletage of her voluminous costume where no policeman or other would dare to inspect. I shall of course have to inform Lestrade at the Yard as soon as I have rested a little, and I shall also send a note to Mr. Greenhalgh.

    He will not like it, but from this evening onwards I suspect it will be the stand-in who will play Mary to Ernest Mason's Jack. Still, I can to some extent sympathise with the poor wretch. From close to, Watson, and without her corsets, she is nowhere near so young and slim and pretty as her costume and make-up may suggest. It was hard work, hard work indeed last night."

He lay back, clearly seeking a little repose, but the curiosity was burning inside me. I could not just sit back like this, I needed to know more.

"But why did she do it, Holmes? And why your sympathy for the wretch?"

"After so many years on the stage playing other persons I do believe she has quite lost touch with the reality of whom she really is – an ageing and second-rate actress reduced to playing in bathetic melodramas. As Mr. Greenhalgh would probably say, she is as unhinged as those cardboard doors on the stage sets. She has suffered for some time from what is technically known as Post-Dramatic Stress Syndrome. Leading to unbalanced emotions and enhanced rage. And so she shot him. As an artiste would."

"You mean...?" I stammered.

"Yes, yes, it was temperamentally, my dear Watson."

..................................................................

# **THE ROSE OF THE NAMES**

Sherlock snorted at the paper. "Names, Watson!" he said. "What bizarre names some parents give their children!"

I thought of 'Sherlock' but kept quiet, knowing as I did (as I thought) some small part of the troubled history of the names of my friend and his brother Mycroft.

"There is this ambitious, up-and-coming politician, and he is named Winston! Harrumph! Could you ever imagine, say, a string quartet where three of the players are called sensible, honest English names like John, George, Paul and then - well, let us say, a 'Ringo'?"

I couldn't, and readily admitted it.

"A writer called Ronald will be easily overlooked," he continued, staring morosely at the 'Times'. "Call him 'Roald' though, and he is bound to be a success. Or just think of Robert Haggard - everyone would laugh. If he is blessed instead with the ridiculous name 'Rider', then he is a literary sensation. Bah! Piffle! Names, Watson, just strange unchristian Christian names. What's wrong with Tom and Tim, John and Jim, eh?"

"Nothing much," I said. "I am, as you know, myself a 'John H.' Though I do confess, I have often wished my dear mother would have vouchsafed to me what the 'H' stands for. Even on re-reading my own notes all the way through I have never yet found out! Could I be John Herbert? John Horace? That would be nice and Classical. John Harry? I would like that. Much more than Herbert."

"Well there!" Sherlock continued. "Tom, Dick and Harry. Do you know, my old friend, in all our years of acquaintanceship it had never crossed my mind to delve into your other nomenclature? This is indeed an admirable mystery. But pray, why do you not simply drop the offending initial if it causes you so much concern and discomfort?"

69

I was shocked, almost to my core. "What, H-holmes?" I said, emphasising the Aitch. "When I was at school in Heaton it was made <u>very</u> clear to us boys that we should NEVER drop our Aitches and become like effete Southerners! No, no, I shall maintain that initial on my visiting cards and on my brass plate, along with the letters 'M.D.' for which, of course, I do indeed know and appreciate the meaning.

I have often wondered," I went on, "whether my mother intended to recall through my name the memory of one of her deceased ancestors or relatives. My maternal grandfather however was Edward, my deceased uncle, who passed away before I was born, was an Anthony. The trail is, alas, cold."

Sherlock appeared to consider for a moment; I should have realised that there is little that arouses his attention more than the prospect of a trail gone cold and awaiting to be warmed up again like one of Mrs. Hudson's chicken-and-mushroom pies. Then with a grunt he returned to the newspaper.

"Our Kings are all called George and Charles and William and Henry and good English names like that. Even our beloved Consort, though unavoidably of foreign extraction, is Albert. And then there are engineers like George and Robert Stephenson. Timothy Hackworth. No problem there. Daniel Gooch on the 'Western' line. Archibald Sturrock on the 'Northern'. Archibald, I like that name, it has a ring to it somehow. But Isambard? Isambard? Kingdom? I ask you! Where do they get these ideas, Watson, eh? What gets into their heads, these prissy piffling new parents at the christening font? They're not biblical. They're not from the Greek. Why don't the vicars ban these names, eh?"

I confessed my ignorance of the relevant Canonical statutes. Sherlock bit on his pipe, looking further down the list of Births. "Good heavens, if it goes on like this they'll start using place names. I fear in my deepest nightmare for some poor child who shall be baptized at the font with the name

Kensington, or even Chelsea. I suppose Kensington could at least be abbreviated to 'Ken', but, I ask you? Or do you think some addlebrain may ever name his daughter 'Paris'?

Some Americans have now, I understand, for lack of any imagination, taken to calling themselves Something-or-Other Junior or even Something-or-Other the Third. Like petty royalty! Hah! There are, I admit, some perfectly acceptable names of Scottish or Irish provenance – we cannot help that, nor can their bearers, if they truly come from the Celtic fringe.

Though I must say I could never envisage a restaurant becoming famous were it to be called "McPherson' or 'McDonald' or similar.

Now, the Welsh, they have musical names, even if they are impossible to spell and even more impossible to pronounce. Such as hr-hr-hr-" - I was momentarily concerned lest my friend be gagging, choking on his brandy, but he continued "-loyd". Now there's something to stretch the tonsils. Or Merlin – there's a name to conjure with. Then we have the foreigners like Mr. Disraeli – but at least he has the decency to have the biblical 'Benjamin' as his, well, can we say 'Christian name'? I believe, you see, that even Hebrews and Mussulmen should have good Christian names, by which I mean, names taken from the Holy Scriptures. Such as David or Paul, Daniel or Joseph, Reuben or even, at a pinch, Jacob. "

Sherlock had rarely shown much interest in religious matters, so I wondered – as a medical man – whether the brandy was perhaps affecting his mental faculties at this point. "Like Beelzebub, perhaps?" I asked and immediately regretted it.

He was launched onto this topic for the evening, I could see, and there was little I could do save reach over for the port decanter and then take out one of my new mild Sturgee cigars to aid in digestion.

"Do you recall that time we took the train from Munich to Vienna, Watson?" he asked, the 'Times' now folded on his knee, as he filled himself yet another large crystal tumbler of the excellent brandy my friend always kept at hand. "For cooking," he used to say in explanation, "you see, I am always cooking up something, in my head!" Yes, I recalled that journey; it had been a singularly unpleasant one, as we had had to change trains at Braunau, an unprepossessing hamlet, after crossing the metal bridge from – where was it now? Somewhere still in Bavaria. Ah yes, Simbach. And it had been a February evening, dank and dark, and we had been in a hurry to rescue a lady's honour – as usual. If only the ladies concerned would do as much to save their own honour, I sometimes reflected, we would not have up to a half of the clientèle.

"Yes, I recall it," I said, with a shudder. "How could I forget? There was that ghastly unpleasant Customs official who wanted to check and note down all your medical powders, I recall. Wouldn't take my word as a Doctor. And he made us miss the connection to Linz. And there was nowhere warm to sleep.

I recall we were told we could not even return to Simbach, even though there were some Inns there – not surprising I suppose, since it is situated on the River Inn. He almost smiled, I recall, when he told us that the Customs Post was now closed until the passage of the Bummelzug at 8 o'clock the next morning. What a bumptious wretch! So we had to huddle on a bench on that awful station."

"Yes, Herr Schekelgrüber – poor chap, I wondered at the time whether his unpleasant and inquisitive nature might have had something to do with his name. It means in German, of course, one who digs constantly for Shekels. A most unpleasant connotation. Implying also an Hebraic past. I remember our conversation distinctly – I said to him, to distract him from his invasive interrogation, that he should perhaps change his profession and become, say, an Hotelier – there was no reasonable hotel there at all, that ghastly night – and maybe then he could change his name to Hotelier too.

I wonder whether he ever did so? It must be awful to have to go through life being called 'Schekelgrüber.' I'm sure his son, should he ever have one, would be much happier to be called 'Herr Hotelier' when he grows up. Though the blasted chap with his dreadful patois accent did keep pronouncing it "Hoiteler.' Of course, just being Austrian is a handicap in itself. Imagine living in a country whose very name begins with an Umlaut! I shudder at the thought." He had now downed his third or maybe even fourth brandy and was clearly warming to his theme as the brandy was warming him too.

"Names, names! How much they tell us, often without people even realising it. Think of Claire Voyant, who developed a lucrative line in premonitions – largely because the client had to pay the money up front before her performance, hence the term pre-moneytions. Then there was Bill Board, the inventor of the advertising hoardings. And so many others."

Suddenly he looked up, an inquisitive look in his eyes. "My good fellow," he said, "I neglected to ask you, when you were speaking some little time ago, the Christian name of your paternal grandfather. Or indeed of your father."

I had been secretly dreading this moment for some time. "The fact is," I began, "I never knew my father. And I am not quite sure whether even my mother knew who my father was. I gather, you see, that there were several candidates for the position."

Holmes looked thoughtful. "I see," was all he would say, though what he could see, I could not myself see.

It was several days later that, after dinner, Holmes broached the subject again. "I have some information for you, my friend," he said. "I trust it will be helpful."

"What?" I asked, utterly confused.

"Well, you see, this little conundrum concerning your middle initial set me off on some investigations. It is indeed quite remarkable what one can find in various archives and libraries, if one knows where to look and whom to ask, and of course, if one takes the time. But I became quite fascinated by the search. By the hunt. (That reminds me, who is this 'Holman' Hunt? There is even a Colonel 'Holman' Stephens. How strange. Not even 'Holy Men.' But I digress.)

Knowing as I do your date of birth, I set off in search in the Newspaper Library yesterday morning. It took me some time, as I was unsure at first which newspaper I should be following up - the 'North Briton', the 'Newcastle Bugle', the 'Heaton Chronicle', but eventually it was in the 'North Shields Tribune' that I found something relevant. It was a remarkable story that was reported there. It seemed that a barque, the "John H." registered to Charleston in the United States, had spent some time in the harbour having intended to deliver, I believe, not just coals but also coke to Newcastle. This was slightly under a year before your date of birth, and so I wondered of course whether there might have been some connection between these two facts.

It is merely an assumption that the 'John H.' is a reference to John Henry – an heroic figure in American folklore, it seems, a freed slave who became a mighty railroad builder or some such, though another entry in my scrap books refers to a John Henry who was a Governor of Maryland some time ago. Of course, my assumption may be wholly wrong and you must admit, my friend, though this is in no way intended as an insult, that the forenames 'John' and 'Henry' are common in the extreme. At least for boys.

To deliver coals to Newcastle is of course a metaphor for a totally pointless exercise and the newspaper reported that the Captain had not fully understood his instructions, which had been to deliver the coal to Newcastle in New South Wales, Australia. He had instead merrily set off across the Atlantic and come to the wrong place.

In any case the loading facilities for coal here are all based upon gravity and he would have had difficulty in unloading at any of the staithes along the Tyne or indeed the Wear.

So the ship was forced to wait a while in the harbour at North Shields until the muddle was sorted out and new provisioning arranged. As they had no money, the men of the crew were put up in a Seamen's Hostel for several days, whilst the officers were, it is reported, graciously offered home hospitality by members of St. Stephen's Parish. The Captain, it stated, lodged with a Mrs. Doris Watson, of 6, Harbour View."

"But, but!" I cried; "That was my home address! Doris is, or was my beloved mother!"

"So I had surmised. The ship eventually left and, from all I could gather from a brief look further through the back numbers, was not referred to ever again. It may, due to its Captain's rather idiosyncratic form of Navigation, have ended up in New Guinea, Newfoundland, New Zealand, who knows?"

"You mean – it vanished?"

"Quite so, it seems. Then in the afternoon I went to Somerset House. It appeared from what I unearthed here that a Mrs. Doris Watson of Harbour View, North Shields, gave birth to a healthy bonny baby boy on - well, I am sure you know the date well enough. And the name given was, curiously, 'John H.' Before you ask, Watson, no, I'm afraid that the column for the father's name was left blank.

So you see, my friend, that despite an extensive search and despite unearthing some quite extraordinary coincidences, we have come but little further in your own quest for your identity. The 'H' remains unresolved and, since your mother is no longer here to tell us more, and the Captain of the ship in question may be by now a good acquaintance of the Welsh-sounding Davy Jones, I fear we shall get no further."

I was astounded by this sudden new information as to my origins, which had been so long veiled and cast in shadow. For a moment it seemed that the shadow might have been lifted – but no, things remained as confused and inchoate as they had been when, as a young Heaton Grammar School scholarship boy, commuting by train and tram each morning from North Shields, I had been taunted by my fellow scholars when I could not tell them what my father did for a living.

"I am most grateful to you, Holmes," I said, "for taking this effort. I confess that for some years now the matter had not occupied my mind so much as it had when I was a boy. The medical training and my time in the Army had left me little time for such idle speculations."

"You mean, What Father, not What Son, eh, Watson?"

I considered this jibe to be in poor taste but, in the circumstances, was not in a position to show ingratitude. Instead I began to write down on a pad of paper the remarkable story he had just recounted.

After an hour or so Holmes put down the 'Times' and looked over to where I was just finishing my manuscript.

"You can call it 'The Marchbanks Mystery'," he said.

"But there is no-one called Marchbanks involved!" I protested.

"Aha," he said, filling his meerschaum pipe once again. "That, my dear Watson, is the Mystery!"

---

## **DEATH AND TAXES**

I had rarely seen my old friend Holmes so upset. "Just look at this, Watson!" he said, throwing an official-looking letter at me. A brief glance showed me why he was so aroused. Some malicious official from the Department of Customs and Revenue had composed a letter to my friend so insulting, so insinuating of malpractice and wrongdoing and betrayal of the interests of the Kingdom and Her Blessed Majesty herself! As my readers will be aware, Sherlock Holmes operated for many years a practice from private rooms in 221B Baker Street and from these premises was able to employ – on a cash basis - a whole swathe of housekeepers, pages, narks, spies, messengers, informants and others. We had regularly to jump at short notice onto trains that took us – First Class of course – to obscure stations in Essex and Dartmoor, to Brixton and Lewisham, to Winchester and Camford, to the Continent..... and to overnight at local hotels of all classes from the luxurious to the usurious, from the best to the bestial, from the desirable to the despicable. Holmes was constantly sending telegrams and taking Hansom cabs to wherever we were most urgently needed. And it need hardly be said that at no time did he pause to request a receipt for such services rendered – if indeed the business was such a one as to permit of anyone ever writing a receipt.

Corpses especially are not renowned for their generosity, even when one has brought their murderer to justice. On many an occasion Holmes sent a discreet letter after completing the solution to a complex case and requested a suitable Honorarium for his unique but not always so valued services.

On other occasions grateful fathers or husbands or widows (it was interesting how often the widows were so especially grateful) would press discreet sums of money into my friend's hand, either in the form of gold specie, coins of many different countries and currencies, or large white bank notes, occasionally even a cheque drawn upon Coutts or one of the other banks used by the nobility.

Often, he refused to demand or accept any payment at all for a relatively simple case involving persons with but limited means. "It is the chase I enjoy," he would then say, "Money is not and never should be a factor!"

Yet my friend lived modestly and within his means and rarely complained even if, as sometimes happened, payment was not forthcoming. It was not his way to send repeated reminders or threats, he relied upon a client's honour and it was only rarely that he was totally deceived and disappointed. But such is the fate of all those who are self-employed. There were months when he was up to his ears in work with maybe three or four difficult cases to be investigated simultaneously, and months when there seemed to be little to do except read the newspapers in hope of encountering some mystery, smoking endless pipes, performing obscure chemical experiments upon his apparatus, reviewing and glueing new items into his vast collection of scrap books, playing melancholic pieces – especially Hoffmann's Barcarolle – endlessly upon his Stradivarius and staring out of the window at the gloomy, dank, grey summer skies.

Yet now this Mr. B. L. Simpson – the very name indicating the character of the person – had sent him a letter which, in official but officious, even bullying tones, begged to remind Mr. Holmes that he had not submitted an Income Tax return for his business for the previous thirteen years and that steps would be taken – exactly which steps were not specified, they were unlikely to be the steps up to the gibbet but it was implied that they would be almost as bad – to distrain upon his goods and chattels unless he were able to demonstrate convincingly and above all speedily the exact nature and extent of his business, his income, his expenses and other disbursements, and of course to provide written receipts for all such.

"Confound it!" shouted Holmes, almost throwing his blackened pipe onto the floor. "It is damnable, damnable! How on earth am I to specify my earnings without revealing the names and identities of my clients, many of whom I have sworn never to reveal? You will recall, Watson, what you wrote once some time ago in your introduction, to, what was it now? Ah yes, that diabolical mystery of the suicidal murderous mad woman at Thor Bridge. If I recall correctly, you mentioned there – no, one moment, let me look it up, I would rather have your exact words."

He moved some pages in one of the large scrap books, searching eagerly, then exclaimed, "Ah yes, here it is. Here is how you began that tale – so you see, Watson, I DO read your accounts, sometimes with a view to seeing if I can recognise the same sequence of events in my own recollection as you do in yours. Now, you wrote in 'The Problem of Thor Bridge' - 'Somewhere in the vaults of the bank of Cox and Co., at Charing Cross, there is a travel-worn and battered tin dispatch-box' (spelled wrong, alas!) 'with my name, John H. Watson, M.D. Late Indian Army, painted upon the lid. It is crammed with papers, nearly all of which are records of cases to illustrate the curious problems which Mr. Sherlock Holmes had at various times to examine. Some, and not the least interesting, were complete failures, and as such will hardly bear narrating' (I do wish you hadn't published that bit, my friend), 'since no final explanation is forthcoming....' right, blah blah, let me see, Mr. James Phillimore, yes, the cutter *Alicia*, yes, I recall that, the disappearance, ah, here is what I was looking for.

'Apart from these unfathomed cases, there are some which involve the secrets of private families to an extent which would mean consternation in many exalted quarters if it were thought possible that they might find their way into print. I need not say that such a breach of confidence is unthinkable, and that these records will be separated and destroyed now that my friend has time to turn his energies to the matter.' Hmm. Well, Watson, what do you think?"

I confessed that I was unable once again to follow his trail of thought.

"My friend, you are so slow sometimes. I confess that on a day like this, when I am already so irritated by the suspicions of officialdom, I had hoped you would be quicker off the mark. But I recall you wrote elsewhere in similar manner. Let me see...."

He turned to his bookshelf and, running his finger along a row of green and white books with a black and white rather surprised-looking Penguin printed distinctively upon each paper cover and spine, picked one battered volume out and flicked through. "Yes, here, as I recalled – it is amazing what one can recall, Watson, when the times are desperate and the 'Times' itself provides no comfort or stimulus – here, in a tale you dramatically entitled 'The Adventure of the Veiled Lodger' – a wholly excessive use of the term 'adventure', I vouch, for all we did was to track down the history of a poor woman who had been mauled by a lion, the woman herself having been, so to speak, delivered into our hands by her landlady; One might well say that the lion's share of the work had been done by... but no, that is in poor taste, even for today. Listen, Watson, here is your Introduction once more:

'When one considers that Mr. Sherlock Holmes was in active practice for twenty-three years, and that during seventeen of these I was allowed to co-operate with him and to keep notes of his doings, it will be clear that I have a mass of material at my command. The problem has always been, not to find, but to choose. There is the long row of year-books which fill a shelf, and there are the dispatch cases filled with documents' (Once again, Watson, you have mis-spelled 'despatch'), 'filled with documents, I repeat, a perfect quarry for the student not only of crime, but of the social and official scandals of the late Victorian era.

Concerning the latter, I may say that the writers of agonized letters, who beg that the honour of their families or the reputation of famous forbears may not be touched, have nothing to fear.

The discretion and high sense of professional honour which have always distinguished my friend are still at work in the choice of these memoirs, and no confidence will be abused.'

And look, I was right, I thought I had recalled it. You go on, 'I deprecate, however, in the strongest way the attempts which have been made lately to get at and destroy these papers. The source of these outrages is known, and if they are repeated, I have Mr. Holmes' authority for saying that the whole story concerning the politician, the lighthouse and the trained cormorant will be given to the public. There is at least one reader who will understand.' That's it, Watson! There are in fact many readers who would understand, were we, were you, to publish this tale in an appropriate way."

"How do you mean, appropriate?" I asked him. I was becoming concerned at the state of my friend's nerves, the way he paced restlessly around the room, the fact that he was filling his third pipe before even finishing the second.

"Why, I am in need of money, Watson!" he said. "Money. Cash. And substantial sums of the same, I would guess, though I have not yet received the Final Demand from this fiend in his grey suit and with his vile pen nib that he always tilts to the left side and the official blue-black ink that, and this is no irony, reflects the blue-black souls of those who use it and always clots when the clots use it. Just look at the way he writes and crosses his 't's! And that Nought – it has been written clockwise! Who writes their noughts clockwise, eh? From his noughts and crosses I would estimate him to be a man of early middle age, a slight cramp in his right shoulder and through fear of his colleagues or superior or maybe his family he has not yet been able to come out openly with his homoerotic fantasies.

It will be vital, and soon, to have a substantial sum of money at my disposal, and not entrapped and recorded in my bank account, for when this demand comes, I shall have but two options.

One, my friend, would be to flee, to change my identity yet again but this time permanently and perhaps seek a quiet retirement, not in my little house on the South Downs but in Switzerland, perhaps, or maybe in contrast the Low Countries, where the supply of cocaine is more assured and the prices not quite so high."

"And the other?" I enquired, truly shaken now, for this would mean the sudden end of our partnership.

"The other? Why, to pay these illegitimate offspring of drunken bestialists their blood sum and at least be able to continue to live here, enjoying the foggy atmosphere of London and the culinary adventures of Mrs. Hudson, and not to forget, of course, my good friend, your own inestimable company. But I fear the demands of the Excise Office will be high."

I felt but little relieved at this mention of his other possible course of action, for the anger was still burning in his voice. He spoke bitterly.

"Money! What is money? It is a symbol, Watson, only a symbol, a symbol of something which, while itself of no worth whatsoever, for who can eat gold, who can be kept sheltered by paper? – can nevertheless purchase so much that we do indeed value and need. It is perhaps no coincidence that some people name a gold coin a Sovereign, for they make it into their king, and they become its humble and obedient subjects. As we know, the French believe in being Franc about their money, the Germans know it can make a Mark, the Danes – quite remarkably for a monarchy – consider it appropriate to keep Crowns in their trouser pockets, and as for the Americans, they have more Cents than sense. Who else would print 'In God we Trust' on their banknotes? And who are they trying to convince by this theological statement?

If the love of money is the root of all evil, as the so-called Good Book says, then the interest _in_ money is a route to all evil and the interest _on_ money drives speculators into madness and the interest in what other people do with their money, an interest shared by so many of these devils in the taxation office, is surely the very evil itself. How can I describe where we have travelled, to which stately homes and discreet lodgings, without revealing to every nosey clerk in the taxation office the destinations and therefore the personages with which we were concerned? Does he really expect the Chequers Hotel at Camford to issue receipts for lodgings? What about those cases where, in any case, I was travelling under a false identity? It is all too, too ridiculous."

"It is indeed a bad business," I replied to him, handing back the letter. "What are we to do?"

"Well, we can expect little help from Scotland Yard of course," he said, quite bitterly. "They are obsessed there with keeping to the letter of the law. Honestly, Watson, I object to being made out to be dishonest, just because I cannot be bothered with all this damnable fiddling paperwork. It is ironic, is it not, that this time round the missing papers are my own!"

I was silent whilst he filled his fourth pipe and puffed heavily upon the stem, but went over to the sideboard to take a plate of cold scrambled eggs.

"But I believe the solution may already be in our hands, or at least, in the records which we have kept. I may say that one of the most valuable commodities of the present age is secrecy and discretion and I wager that there are many former clients who, whether or not they have reimbursed me in the past for their efforts on their behalfs, would most certainly be prepared to pay now for some further guarantee. In which case I should be in a position to accumulate the funds that these demons in the taxation office demand from me.

Death and Taxes, Watson! These are the only certainties in life, and right now, after confronting the former already on several occasions, I tend towards preferring the latter. But it will be dear, oh yes, it will be a merry sum that I shall require. So I shall turn along this path only if it be absolutely necessary."

At this moment there came a ring at the door downstairs and the sound of Mrs. Hudson's hob-nailed boots clumping upon the hall floorboards. "Aha!' said Holmes, "This may be a visitor I am expecting, indeed, whom I have summoned." A few moments later the door was opened and a grey-clad person entered the room, tall, with long dark hair, a dark complexion and a slight moustache. It was only at the second glance and a look at the clothing that one realised the nature of the person.

"Please be seated," said Holmes, indicating the usual armchair, which meant that from where I was standing, I could see only their back – which made his following remarks rather redundant for me. "Watson, you will observe the callus upon the right thumb and the two ink stains upon the right hand and the sleeve, both blue-black and red. These are the colours used most frequently in her work – alas, you will see that there is more red than blue-black, thus reflecting the level of the current economy.

She requires to wear spectacles for close reading – mark the indentation upon the bridge of her nose. You are, madam, as I can easily see, a person with a constant grimace upon your features and all the signs of one who lacks the joys of life and sees little reason why others should then also enjoy it. This, Watson, is Miss Gwendolene Sharples. She is, Watson, believe it or not, an Accountant!"

Like many a woman, a species with whom I have had relatively little contact and that at my own desire, my own dear wife Mary forming the sole exception to the rule, she looked best from behind – her long brown hair spread gently over her shoulders and made her look exceedingly mysterious and almost attractive.

It was only when she turned around to face me that one saw the protruding forehead, the sharp nose, the large wart or pimple high on her right cheek under the eye, and the lack of a smile. Was she perhaps, I wondered, one of those women born to be a thorn amongst roses? One who had therefore decided to lessen the burden of her single and tedious and unrewarding life by learning a profession, one where she might do her utmost to prevent, as Holmes had said, others from being carefree and happy?

"Miss Sharples," said Holmes, "I am facing incessant and threatening demands from the Income Tax office. They demand papers, papers and more papers, papers which I do not have. Is there anything you can suggest?"

At this point I swallowed the last of my eggs and announced that I would take my leave, for this was a subject upon which I also confessed to little knowledge and less interest. Before I left however Holmes said to me, quite sharply, "I'd be obliged though if you could come round tomorrow at ten. And bring any notes you have with you." I acquiesced and departed, leaving the two in animated conversation.

Next morning I was shaking the rain from my cape at the appointed time and ascended the stairs to find my friend seemingly plunged once more in gloom. But he rose with a sudden, almost manic, smile when he saw me. "Watson!" he said, "So good of you to come. Did you bring your notes?"

I indicated the leather despatch case I had brought with me. He rubbed his hands in anticipatory glee and leaned forward to take it from me.

"I regret to say," he said, "that Miss Sharples was unable to proffer a great deal of useful advice. Or anything else, for that matter. I had hoped that such an unusual creature as a female member of that ignoble profession might have turned out to be more, shall we say, flexible in her interpretation of certain regulations. But such turned out not to be the case. So we remain with our problem."

I expressed some words of comfort, but he brushed them aside. "Fear not, Watson, for I believe I have the solution here, in my hand," and he raised the leather case. "You will recall what I read for you yesterday, how we have until now promised not to reveal any identities of specific clients – clients who, if we are honest about this, are precisely those who most value the fact that we have not done so, and would therefore be most likely to appreciate in pecuniary terms the extension of that grace. And who are indeed those most well situated to make such monetary sums worth pursuing and accepting."

I was horrified. "You mean, Blackmail?" I cried.

"Well, if we need to raise a substantial sum of money quickly in order to pay off these outrageous demands of officialdom, then we shall need to contact some of these Principals. Can't afford mere principles, eh? And though the banknotes be white, the business itself is often black.

My suggestion is this. Sit down, good fellow, and compose one more of your worthy tales, but this time indicate to the readers that I face financial ruin unless those clients who continue to value my discretion find some means of sending me sums, appropriate sums, to alleviate my situation. If not, we shall be compelled to raise funds by continuing with a further series of my Adventures in the 'Strand' magazine or any other publication, but this time revealing All. Those who wish to retain their Seats – whether their country seats or their parliamentary ones – will now need to make up for my lack of re-ceipts. Yes, let the readers tremble, until with quivering hands they find their purses, their wallets, their socks under the mattress, all those hiding places of which we know – yet they do not know that we know – and open them wide. Let them express their gratitude in practical generosity. Now, indeed, is the time for all men (good and not-so-good) to come to the aid of this particular party. I have no reverence for the Revenue, but I must clear my debts. The alternatives, I have already explained."

I was astounded but could see indeed the hard logic of his solution. There were many who owed him money and many who owed him favours and many who owed him both and if, as he said, the situation was as desperate as he had made out, then something would have to be done.

"Make it clear," said Holmes, staring out of the window and rubbing his hands, "That if they send an appropriate sum – coins by messenger, though banknotes by post will suffice – and I am sure we can leave the actual amounts to their discretion - then we will send in return the copy of your notes on their specific case. All right? Of course, when I say 'Copy' I mean precisely this, for there is no telling when such a need may arise once more in the future, eh? Always keep a copy for us as well."

I nodded. "But will we always be able to match up specific payments to specific cases?" I asked.

"Well, you have an entry for each case in your lengthy Index, is that not so?" he asked.

I nodded once more, having always been proud of my systematic filing system, took out my fountain pen and sat at his writing-desk. Clearly this was an urgent commission.

"Well, Watson, that's what we'll do. Inform them that each has an entry in your extensive notebooks, which may be individually and indeed exclusively acquired."

"And then?" I enquired, not quite clear what he was getting at.

"Why, sell 'em an entry, my dear Watson," responded Holmes, more cheerful now, and lit his pipe.

............................................................

## SHERLOCK - GO HOME.

In all the many years since I first brought to the attention of the world the deeds of my dear friend and companion Sherlock Holmes, there has been one phrase which has always attracted attention - even though, according to some critics, it was never actually uttered. In fact - and this is what I wish to place on record with this account - it <u>was</u> uttered, but only once, and in circumstances such that even I, his long-standing and faithful recorder, could not bring myself to publish them until now.

It was, I recall, one winter's evening in late November. Mrs. Hudson had cleared away the dinner things and, looking from the window of 221B Baker Street, the dense fog outside our rooms was matched only by the dense fug inside as my friend settled down to his third pipe of the evening - for he was tackling, indeed, a mighty and complex problem. We were tired, for we had already had a very busy and adventurous week in which we - I include myself in only a modest capacity, of course - had succeeded in regaining some vital stolen papers, thus averting a threatened war with China and preserving the honour of a Very Important Lady - all this, I am glad to say, without the injurious necessity of dispatching any innocent canine moorland creatures and thus antagonising the Literary Animal Rights lobby.

At last my friend put down his 'Times', groaning in despair. "One Down, Watson!" he cried, "One Down!" I confess I was puzzled, for his words made no sense. One what? Down where? On my enquiry, he jabbed a long finger at the crumpled newspaper at his feet. On retrieving it I found that he had been unable to resolve one of the clues in the paper's noted Crossword Puzzles - most unusually for him, and a clear sign of his mental exhaustion. The clue read, as I still recall, "Plough with a Wealdstone; 6 letters."

"Harrow!" I ejaculated, unthinkingly, for it always annoyed him excessively when I found an answer before him.

"Harrow, of course!" And reaching for our trusty Bradshaw I showed him where Harrow and Wealdstone station lay proudly on the North-Western line.

It was unlike my friend to utter the words which proceeded at this point from his mouth, through clenched teeth. He almost bit off his pipe stem in rage. But, when he had calmed down sufficiently and taken a further glass of port, he told me, "What a fool I am, Watson! I should have known that. You see, I went to school there."

I was surprised, but not amazed. In all the years we had worked together, never once had my friend spoken of his childhood or his youth. Ever the perfect English gentleman, it was clear that he had enjoyed a sound, nay an excellent education, for his regular allusions to matters both Classical and scientific bore witness to wide reading as well as deep analysis. But he had never told me of his School, had never worn a specific Tie or spoken of a Club or mentioned a Reunion or in any other way indicated which School he had attended. And so, since he was clearly prepared to open up on this subject, I decided to ask further.

"So you were at Harrow?" I asked, casually. "I'm a Repton man myself, don'tye'know."

"Of course, I know," he responded. "I knew the moment we first met, those many years ago. You wore your jacket with the left cuff creased over the elbow; the third finger of your left hand still bore the stains of the special blend of indelible Blue-Black ink that only Repton College and Shrewsbury use, and only at Repton are the ink-wells on the left side of the writing desks. But the main clue, I have to confess, was the badge upon your blazer, the badge worn by the Repton Second-Eleven."

I was, naturally, speechless with amazement. "You have known all this time? But why have you never mentioned your own School?"

A look of pain, a quick twinge or grimace, flashed across his aquiline features. "It is not something I have ever desired to discuss, my dear Watson," he said.

"But why be so ashamed of Harrow?" I asked. "Was there something.... well, something beastly there?"

He pulled the decanter of Port towards him and took, most unusually, another large glass. "You will not find the name of Sherlock Holmes on the Rolls of Harrow School. If you listened carefully, my friend," he said, "I did not say that I went to Harrow School but that I went to school in Harrow. There is a difference."

He sighed, and then went on, "But I suppose, after all these years and all these adventures, you deserve to know the truth."

Looking deeply into the fire, he then proceeded to tell me a most astonishing tale. "With my father but a few years into his well-deserved Life Sentence at Dartmoor, when the syphilis and the gin began to get to my mother, my brother and I were taken by well-meaning relatives into care. They soon decided that we were perhaps a little too advanced in our tastes for their own household - I had been taking cocaine regularly for three years by this time and, as for my brother, well, I can only say that it is lucky for all of us that there is a Foreign Office. So - we were each sent to an Institution. As it happens, a special Home for boys of our age and predilections. There we soon learned the meaning of discipline and were only too happy to put our pasts well behind us, and our identities too - indeed, we were encouraged in this by the authorities at the Homes. So, on leaving to join the Navy, both my brother and I decided to take the names of our respective places of residence and, so to speak, make a clean start.

I had been at the Alderman Sherlock Home in Preston Road and he had been at the Councillor Mycroft Home in Kenton. It was but a tiny matter to Anglicize the surname into "Holmes", but now at least you have the explanation for our rather unusual forenames too - a matter which, I know, has bothered some of your readers for quite a while."

"But... but...." I was almost struck dumb. "But where were you educated?"

"At the Board School on Bessborough Road, Harrow," he smiled back at me. "They were, I might say, actually amongst the happiest days of my life."

"But what sort of school was it?" I expostulated.

He sighed, and answered in those famous words:

"Elementary, my dear Watson."

-------------------------------------------

# THE INSEED JOB

It was a dank summer's day as we received a most unusual visitor and commission. Mrs. Hudson led to our door a gentleman of middle age, clad in a relatively formal suit which was, however, stained and smeared with soil, and who seemed of a most nervous disposition. Holmes had been spending part of the afternoon on some of his obscure and pungent chemical experiments in the small room at the rear but he came out when I summoned him, cast our visitor a glance and said, "Ah, I see we have here a gardener, but no, more than a gardener, perhaps a researcher, a plant biologist? In which case I would be prepared to wager, from the Royal Botanic Gardens in Kew. Am I right?"

Our visitor sank, nay, almost collapsed into the armchair behind him, his face muscles working uncontrollably, but then he gathered himself together and stood once more and bowed to Holmes and briefly to me. "G-g-g-good heavens, man, b-b-b-but how did you work that out?"

"Well," said Holmes, "It is apparent to me at once that you enjoy gardening, your trousers and the tips of your boots reveal you spend a lot of time kneeling, not in a church but in a field or a flower bed, the left knee shows traces more of some fibrous compost than of soil, your metal-rimmed spectacles reveal you to be more of an academic than, say, a commercial market gardener or a mere amateur potterer with pots, and so, although there are several Plant Biological Institutes and universities at which you could be engaged, I simply chose to mention the most local and most prestigious. That you have part of a District Railway return ticket in your hat band was, I confess, an additional clue."

"Well, well, well, remarkable. May I please p-present you with my card," and he did so. "I am, as you see, Professor Arbuthnot Waterbutt and I am indeed, as the numerous initials will tell you, a Fellow of several Learned Societies, though this is not why I came to see you today." I knew that Holmes had been secretly hoping for some time to be invited into membership of one of these Societies, admission to which is by invitation only, so I was sure he felt keen disappointment at this last sentence.

"Well," said Holmes, "Your card indeed tells us a lot about you, but not, I fear, what it is we can do for you. What is the matter upon which you have come so suddenly?"

The Professor glanced at his soiled trousers, blushed slightly and began. "It is the Honey, Mr. Holmes, the special Honey. It appears that Kew Gardens has been infiltrated somehow and some seed has been stolen, some special seed, and we need to find out how this has occurred."

"Intriguing," said Holmes, lighting a pipe. "Please tell us more. Oh no, not yet, I almost forgot - I still have a Bunsen burning in the other room; I was interrupted by your arrival." He left the room hurriedly and the professor and I heard a cry of exasperation and a small explosion and some tinkling glass, then a silence, during which we looked helplessly at each other, before Holmes returned. "Oh well," he said, "It was only low-grade stuff anyway. Yellowcake. Not very radioactive. Mrs. Hudson can clear it up afterwards when she dusts. Now then, Professor, please continue from where we were, no, from the beginning, if you please."

"Very well, Mr. Holmes. It concerns the Milonesian Poppy. I doubt if you have heard of it."

"But I have!" exclaimed Holmes. "I believe, though, that it is extinct. From one of the Milonesian Islands, yes? A poppy whose seeds made a honey that had opiate qualities as well?"

"I am surprised and impressed, Mr. Holmes. Few indeed have heard even of the Milonesian Archipelago, in the South Seas, let alone of the Poppy. But it is not extinct. It is now some fifty-five years since the archipelago was first discovered, towards the end of a long and tiring and, I believe, rather frustrating expedition by a team of young scientists from one of our older universities, with the assistance of the

Royal Navy. The consequence of what I have just mentioned is that the islands are named, respectively, ahem, "Bluddijungle", "Morebluddijungle", "Yetmorbluddijungle" and "Coraltipnjungle". They appear so on the larger-scale charts. They were uninhabited, except of course by a few natives, who don't count, and so were claimed for our then-new great beloved Queen.

I do wish, by the way, that our scientific expeditions were sometimes a little more, shall we say, serious-minded? These young men seem to think that, just because they have gone over the horizon, certain standards may slip. Maybe they become unhinged by the endless horizons of the oceans. We have an Easter Island, discovered on Easter Day, and a Christmas Island, so named for the same reason – I am personally surprised that anything could be discovered on what is, after all, a Bank Holiday as well as a religious festival. But recently we received a crate of unusual plants from Second-Sunday-in-Advent Island. I had never heard of the place.

Well, to return to my theme, it appeared that there were few if any natural resources of any commercial worth on these lonely outcrops in the ocean, but the expedition team did notice one specific species of poppy which the natives had explained produced a pollen which, when gathered by the local bee population, made a delicious and soothing honey.

Several of the expedition's members consumed some of this honey, some also imbibed a form of primitive mead made from this honey, and from this point on their Log becomes largely unreadable, decorated with often tasteless sketches, but it was clear that after a lengthy initial period of slumber they awoke to find they had lost almost all interest in further scientific endeavour. So they dug out several specimens of this plant, a form of yellow poppy, and brought it back with them to England, where in due course it found its way to our Institute. The then-Director decreed that it should be kept for scientific purposes only and in one of the more secure glasshouses and this rule was strictly adhered to. You will understand, Mr. Holmes, that it is our scientific duty to maintain for purposes of research several plant species which are, in fact, forbidden for public consumption."

"Yes," said Holmes, his eyes gleaming. "And so some seeds survived, did they? By jingo."

"Indeed. Mr. Holmes, not only did they survive but they flourished and in fact still do, largely at present due to my own tender care of the plants, though of course I can only build upon the efforts of my predecessors. However, it has recently come to our attention that Lord Brierley of Brierley Hall in Norfolk is now marketing a form of honey which, from its description, must be manufactured from the pollen gathered from the Milonesian Poppy. The Director of the Botanical Institute in Kew now wishes to find out how, if this is so, the Poppyseeds were taken or smuggled out of Kew. For me, personally, this is also important as, I need hardly tell you, unless some other culprit is to be found, the finger of suspicion rests also upon me and this could severely damage my career. I can of course assure you, Mr. Holmes, that I am wholly innocent in this matter. Yet we are totally at a loss to understand how these seeds could have got to Norfolk. Can you assist us?"

"I shall try," said Holmes. "Watson and I shall come down to Kew this very afternoon, indeed, we may be able to gather ourselves together quickly and come with you now. Let us start our researches at the scene of the crime, as it were."

With little further ado Holmes had donned his cape and deerstalker, packed his notepad and magnifying glass, and we set off through the drizzle to Baker Street station, from where we took a train around the Circle line until we could change into a District Railway train for Richmond via Kew Gardens. We were introduced to and welcomed officially by the Director in his commodious offices which were, I noted, filled with indoor plants, and were handed over to an Assistant Keeper, Morgan, who had the keys to what were termed "The Special Houses". Professor Waterbutt had other duties to attend to and in any case, he had explained to us during the journey that, due to the fact that he was also under suspicion, he would probably not be entrusted to show us the scene himself.

Morgan was an elderly man with many years of experience, that was clear. We walked for quite some distance past many rows of glasshouses and through several gaps in high stone walls into new and different enclosures. "Don't throw any stones here, Watson," murmured Sherlock to me as we made our way past further rows of cold frames. Eventually we came to a long glasshouse, almost hidden behind tall dark bushes, and here Morgan extracted a large bunch of keys and employed three to open different locks on the door.

The Milonesian Poppy was unmistakeable, its plants largely filled a raised bed along one side. It was tall with yellow-orangey petals and bore not only leaves of a pungent green but several unripe rounded seed-pods too. The air was filled with a sweet smell.

"Aha!" said Holmes. "Until now Biology has not been one of my main interests, but I do indeed have a smattering of knowledge. Let us first observe, and then ask." Taking out his magnifying glass he began to study the plant, its stalk, its foliage, its blossoms, the seed pods and more; he prodded a leaf with his fingers. "Interesting," he said; "It is almost odourless. See"- and with a look at Morgan, who gave a gruff nod, he plucked a leaf and placed it under my nose.

"Then what is that smell?" I asked, for the air was thick with the musk of perfumed plants.

"Oh, fear not, Watson, look behind you. Those are the "Too-Sweet Peas" – also liable, if the leaves are smoked, to make you high 'toute-suite', as the French say. Best to keep away from them, I'd say. You must mind your Peas and Kews here."

He then walked several times up and down the glasshouse, peering closely at the windows and window-catches, the heating pipes and other apparatus, and the locks. Eventually he turned to Morgan and said "Thank you, I believe we are finished here for now. Just one question – who has access to this Glasshouse normally?"

Morgan thought for a moment. "Well, normally of course it is restricted. There is the Professor, naturally, and three of the Assistant Keepers – Mr. Dickens, Mr. Price and Herr Dr. Spindelegger – he is a highly qualified Botanist, but a foreigner, and so he is just an Assistant - and myself."

"You said 'Normally' just now," said Holmes, pouncing upon the man's words. "What about when it is not normal?"

"Well," said Morgan, "There are the Open Days, of course. Once a year, the Public is allowed access. By which I mean, also to the areas which are normally closed to the Public. It was an idea of the new Director, which he introduced some five years ago – I confess, not many of the staff were enamoured of the idea but, well, he IS the Director. And so on the first Sunday in June we open up the workshops and most of the glasshouses and have to be here to display and discuss our work with the lay enthusiasts."

"Here too?" asked Holmes.

"Yes and no. That is to say, the first time, maybe even the first two times, even this section was included. But then Professor Waterbutt complained, said it was too difficult to supervise the public, and he got his way. So Sections L2 and L3 are kept closed now, even on the Open Days."

"But they were opened at least once, maybe twice? Hmmmm," said Holmes, looking thoughtful.

On the way back – we retraced our route but for once Holmes did not insist we let the first two trains pass and take only the third, which was a relief – Holmes pondered at first, puffed at his pipe – we were of course in a Smoking carriage – and then said, "A strange place, Watson."

"In what way?" I asked.

"Well, we are accustomed to looking at a flower bed, say, and thinking that all is peaceful, are we not? But it is not so, Watson, not so at all. It is normally a battlefield. Where we have just been is like a Zoo, except that at a Zoo you can actually see the fierce animals and their teeth and how they walk to and fro, plotting their next mayhem, how they devour the meat thrown into their cages. But plants are no different, really. Nature green in root and straw. Each plant is striving to take the other's light, or water, or to strangle its roots. It all happens so slowly and so quietly that we barely notice it, until suddenly we maybe notice after some years how the mistletoe or the ivy has smothered a tree, or until we see how wild plants, which we call Weeds, are taking over the areas we have planted with our own domesticated plants, which we call Flowers. Nettles, brambles, briars, dandelions, all seek to invade, to set down their own roots at the expense of others. If only we could see it, Watson, we would be amazed at the brutality and the cruelty of this struggle for life. Let your seeds fall in the wrong place, and they have no chance to flourish. Careless stalks cost leaves, blotting out the lives of all the small plants huddled at the bottom of the stalk and kept in the shade until they expire.

It is a veritable battlefield. Have you ever seen the forest floor under a stand of pines? Evergreen above, ever-brown below. Sterilised by these acidic needles they drop on any competitors. Why, I become quite angry when I consider the self-righteousness of these modern Vegetarians! Do they care for the struggle these plants have so they may live? No! How uncaringly they pluck, say, a full-grown carrot from his earthy home and leave him to die, tortured through lack of moisture!

How they slice into cabbages, how they let the life-juice spill from oranges, how they deprive the apple tree of her young, plucking them just as they reach maturity! And yet they boast of their morality? Pshaw!"

He was, indeed, quite angry. "That's the plant world for you, Watson, the vegetable kingdom. The Biologists and Botanists at Kew do their best to research all this, Watson my friend, they pull out what is not intended to grow there, they keep the walls whitewashed to prevent growth of invasive moulds or mosses or other spores, but despite all this weeding and whiting it is a damnably long and slow process and one might need years to see, for example, the results of some cross-breeding experiment. Too slow for me, I confess, I could never do the job. I need to see results more quickly! And speaking of results, I think it is time we should go and investigate Lord Brierley at Brierley Hall."

When we got back to Baker Street and had had our dinner, Holmes said "Pass me the Bradshaw" and buried himself in that work. He emerged a while later, looking discontented. "It appears we will have to use the Great Eastern," he said. "There are few other options – I wouldn't trust the Midland and Great Northern, not at this time of year. Tomorrow, Watson, 9.30 from Liverpool Street!"

The next morning at almost the appointed time the express for Norfolk departed those smokey caverns, with a bright blue locomotive and smart wooden carriages but, for an Express, a distressing tendency to halt rather frequently, to pause at leisure and then restart only slowly. We changed into a branch train hauled by a fussy tank locomotive; We were the only First-Class passengers, the rest having the appearance of yokels and bumpkins and shortly after 2 o'clock, feeling hungry, we arrived at Brierley station. The station was small but seemed rather busy – Holmes walked along the platform to the Luggage Van and observed as several wicker baskets were being loaded into the van.

"Rather a lot of pigeons," he observed to the sweating Porter who was swinging the baskets from a trolley to the Guard, who was receiving and stacking them in his vehicle. "It's His Lordship," wheezed that worthy. "Big pigeon race this afternoon. Just a short one, mind, for the young 'uns, training. These 'as ter be in Cromer afore five." Inside the baskets pigeons of various shades of grey could be observed, chirruping thoughtfully to themselves.

Within minutes the baskets were loaded, the Guard had closed the doors, waved his flag and blown his whistle and the branch train was on its way. We made our way too, to the 'Station Hotel' where we partook of a reasonable ham pie with vegetables and a passable local beer – at least, I believe I passed most of it within an hour. Suitably refreshed and rested, Holmes engaged a local driver to convey us in his trap to Brierley Hall and to wait for us on the road outside while we explored the Estate. "I won't call upon His Lordship," said Holmes. "At least, not unless it is really necessary. In any case, I believe he will be rather busy this afternoon." We walked along the driveway but did not go up to the Hall, instead breaking off and passing through some bushes so as to remain out of view from the Hall's windows. And so we came to the outhouses.

"Aha!" said Holmes and pointed with his stick. I saw it straight away – a largeish enclosed garden, like an Orangery, but filled instead with orange petals.

"The Milonesian Poppies!" I gasped. "No less, Watson," he replied. "And see what else we have here!"

I looked but saw only a rather long row of dovecotes. "At Five, they were being released at Cromer, eh?" said Holmes. "Well then, let us wait, it cannot be very long now."

I was a little uncertain what he meant but he motioned to me to remain silent as a middle-aged man, dressed as scruffily as only a Lord in his own grounds can be, walked with upright bearing along the gravel pathways towards the Dovecotes, sat upon a bench set against a wall and looked into the sky, showing a mixture of patience and expectation. Then he took a small jar from his pocket and what looked like a long spoon, opened the jar, took a spoonful of some thick semi-liquid substance from it, sucked the spoon clean, replaced the lid on the jar and fell into what appeared a deep sleep.

I glanced several times at my watch – it showed just five-thirty when, with a flutter of wings a bird came into the courtyard and the man suddenly sprang up and began almost dancing, waving his arms like wings as though he too were attempting to fly, then cooing to it in terms of endearment, and holding out a hand filled with some sort of seed. The bird came slowly towards him, then fluttered onto his arm, to his obvious pleasure as he stroked it. Then came another, and then another, and within a few minutes there must have been twenty pigeons that had arrived. The man was talking animatedly to each of them in turn, fluttering like a pigeon himself.

"I think we have seen enough," said Holmes quietly. "Let us make our way back."

There was of course no hope of getting back to London that night so we had to put up in (and with) the 'Station Hotel' and following breakfast next morning walk over to the station for the branch train and eventually onto a main-line service back to Liverpool Street. At Brierley on this morning we noticed that several cases labelled 'Funny Honey' were being loaded into the van and at the Junction these cases were conveyed by trolley to the main-line platform for onward conveyance.

We settled down to pass the journey, but once the Guard had come round to check our tickets Holmes suddenly said "Watson – if he comes this way again, please engage the Guard in conversation - anything, you know, delays, connections and so – until I am back, yes?

I must just check on some evidence." And with that he had left the compartment and moved along the corridor.

In fact, to my relief it was not long before he returned, took his seat again and said, "Don't worry, Watson, everything is in order."

On our way back to Baker Street Holmes arranged to send a telegram to Professor Waterbutt, urging him to come and see us at his soonest pleasure. Hardly back ourselves and still unpacking, he arrived and knocked at the door. "Take a seat," said Holmes, "and may I offer you a cup of tea? A small brandy, perhaps? I hope you don't mind my pipe."

"What do you have to tell me?" asked the flustered little man.

"Well, firstly, you can set your Director's mind at ease, my good fellow," said Holmes, almost patronisingly. "Indeed, the irony is that this is all caused by one of his own foolish populist ideas. The Public Open Days. Though how you can express this to him, I shall leave to you."

"I don't understand," he said.

"Well then, let me explain what I have learned. Firstly, you may not have noticed, but there were several streaks of pigeon deposit near one of the windows of the glasshouse containing the Milonesian Poppies. It was dry and encrusted and old, but nevertheless there. I assume that not many pigeons are allowed into the glasshouses?"

"Why. none at all Mr. Holmes!" exclaimed the Professor. "They could cause untold damage! The houses are kept free of such pests as far as possible. Of course, there may be occasions when one manages to flutter in, but if so, it will be expelled as soon as possible!"

"Quite so," said Holmes. "Well, my friend and I went down yesterday to Brierley Hall, to investigate the matter further. On the station we witnessed baskets of homing pigeons being loaded into the train for release elsewhere, and during our stay at the nearby inn we heard from the landlord that His Lordship is widely renowned as a fancier of pigeons, and not of the roasted variety.

On making our way unseen to parts of the Estate at Brierley Hall we found a large plantation of the Milonesian Poppies, with many bees going about their busy business amongst them, making the most of the summer blooms. Interestingly, he grows them in the open, not under glass. They must be hardier than you allow for here."

"So he has them, the scoundrel!" said the Professor. "But how did he get them?"

"That was exactly the point to which I was coming," said Holmes. not too happy at the interruption. "As I have already mentioned, His Lordship is an enthusiast for Homing Pigeons, yes, pigeons which are trained, first through short and then gradually longer flights to make their way back to their home dovecote from wherever they are released, using their homing instincts. We witnessed yesterday how His Lordship, dressed in clothes that even a normal gardener would be ashamed to don, welcomed his returning pigeons, held them, expressed all forms of almost intimate friendship with them as they came, even danced with them.

So my theory is that on that Public Open Day some five years ago Lord Brierley, dressed anonymously as a typically-scruffy gardening enthusiast, attended the event, with at least one or maybe more homing pigeons secreted about his person. Once he had found the glasshouse with the Milonesian Poppies he released it, or them, to allow them to consume some of the seed pods and then eventually make their way out through some gap or window and fly back to Brierley Hall. Here they would have been welcomed – possibly by a lackey, for I am certain they can fly faster than the Great Eastern's expresses and so would have been back before he was - and allowed to rest and to do whatever it is that pigeons do. All he had to do then was to plant the dung and wait and see what grew. He was in this respect fortunate that at least one Poppy came forth from the seeds, from which of course as a good gardener he could easily cultivate more seeds and so expand his plantation.

An insidious and indeed an inside job, as I suspected at the first, though I am myself surprised at the beautiful simplicity of it all."

Professor Waterbutt sat pale-faced and took with trembling hand the tumbler of brandy that my friend now passed to him. "I thank you from the bottom of my heart," he said. "Is there anything I can do for you to reciprocate?"

"No thanks are necessary, my friend," said Holmes, "But possibly an invitation into the Royal Society of Botanists?"

"I'll see what I can do," said the Professor; he drained the tumbler, rose unsteadily, took his hat and left.

After he had gone Holmes smiled and laughed loudly. "Hah!" he said, "That went well, I think. Oh, I forgot, Watson, I have something still." With that he went to his cape, hanging on its customary hook behind the door, and took from a pocket a glass jar which he placed upon the table. "This one's for you, I have another in the other pocket."

"What is it?" I asked. It was filled with a light brown substance.

"Why, a jar of the Funny Honey. You will recall that I arranged for us to take a compartment as close as possible to the Luggage Van on the train from the junction? Well, once the Guard was safely about his other duties, I thought I'd just slip along to the Van and check, don't you know? It didn't take long to lever open one of those cases and remove a couple of specimens for evidence, should such be necessary. I think I'll enjoy mine tomorrow afternoon on some toasted muffins. You saw what it did to the old boy. You too?"

"But I still don't understand," I said. "How did those seeds then get delivered to Brierley Hall? Not on a package attached to a leg or something like that? Like we used to do with messages on carrier pigeons in the Indian Army?"

"No, my friend," said Holmes, and knocked out his pipe in the ashtray. "It wasn't that at all. It was excrementary, my dear Watson."

…...........................

# THE CASE OF THE POWDERED MILK

My friend Sherlock Holmes was, as you may have gathered, a man of many and varied moods and these moods were often influenced, alas, by his pharmacological intake. As a medical and military man I had, of course, seen much of this phenomenon on the North-West Frontier; Many a good man, cooped up for months in a fort in the blazing hills, would go to seed when discipline became slack and one of the seeds they would go to would be that of the opium poppy, traded so generously by the local Pathans. Holmes, too, would go through periods of depression that seemed to be alleviated only by an opportunity to take a little opium, cocaine or other substances, some of which he himself prepared in his ingenious chemical apparatus in the study at 221B Baker Street.

But one evening I was taken rather by surprise when he entered his lodgings in some haste and in a state of some disarray. I had been let in earlier by the estimable Mrs. Hudson and had taken a place by the fire and was perusing a copy of a mildly-amusing journal of some sort - "Punch", I think it was - when he almost burst into the room, still in his outdoor cloak and deerstalker. Noticing me, he said, "Hah! Watson! Excellent! No time to lose! Keep 'em talking, eh?" and before I had time to ejaculate some form of answer, which I was endeavouring to couch in the interrogative, there was the sound of heavy knocking on the door downstairs. "It's a bust, Watson," he told me - a term I did not at that time understand for, whilst it was true that he held a bag in his hand, it seemed an ordinary sort of small paper bag and in no way large or sturdy enough to carry even a small porcelain or bronze bust, or indeed any other ornament.

The knocking downstairs grew louder and more determined, and in the sudden silence that followed we could hear Mrs. Hudson's boots approaching the door. Casting his glance around the room, Holmes issued another short "Ha!" and darted towards the tea tray, upon which Mrs. Hudson had earlier brought me a nice pot of tea with some of her terrible rock buns; There was, of course, a jug of milk and a bowl of sugar on the tray and my friend almost jumped at the table, then emptied the contents of the paper bag - a white powder, I noticed - into the milk jug, stirred it furiously with the spoon, then crumpled up the bag and threw it onto the flames of the fire where it curled up in a mixture of green and purple flame before vanishing; he threw off his hat and cloak, and took the armchair opposite me and picked up his pipe just before our door opened.

Mrs. Hudson was almost propelled into the room by two large Constables, one of whom said, in a deep constabulary voice: "I am Constable Robinson of the Drugs Squad; We have reason to believe, Sir, that certain Controlled Substances are in your possession."

"Eh?" said Holmes, looking up from his hastily-opened newspaper.

"Sir, we have followed to these premises a man wearing a distinctive item of headgear not unlike the one I see on the floor behind your armchair," said the Constable - a remarkable piece of observation and insight for one so low in the promotional ladder, all things considered  - "and we suspect he may have made a purchase of certain substances from a dealer by the name of Harry the Nose, whom we have been keeping under observation now for two days."

"Good heavens!" I expostulated, taking care not to catch Holmes' eye. "You mean, you suspect my friend here of...?" - I had no need to finish the sentence, the man was already prowling around the room in an inquisitorial manner. He looked under a newspaper, picked up the cloak and searched in the rear pockets and even - a poor habit, I thought - sniffed suspiciously at the sugar in the sugar bowl.

"Watson," said Holmes, rising from the armchair; "I shall write a letter - would you please take it round to my good friend Inspector Lestrade at the Yard?"

"Of course," I replied, noticing how our investigator's ears suddenly turned crimson. He turned to us and said, "There is nothing visible, I grant you that; but next time I shall bring my Trained Hound". On this, and without even a civil Goodbye, he turned and, with his colleague who had stayed near the door, left the room. We heard their heavy boots on the steps and Mrs. Hudson closing the outside door behind them.

"A close shave, that, Watson," said Holmes, picking up his cloak and hat and placing them on his chair. "I should have noticed that Harry was more nervous than usual. But, all's well that ends well. I shall now have to find some means of recovering my rather diluted purchase." He picked up the milk jug and looked in it. "Another ten minutes, I should say, and then we can pour the milk slowly from the top, through some filter paper, and dry the rest in a dish over my Bunsen burner. A nuisance, but it cannot be helped."

"Why?" I asked. "How can you recover whatever that infernal powder was?"

"Oh, that is no problem, my good friend," he replied, with his disarming smile. "The solid will separate from the liquid, given time and assistance. The solution is, you see, Sedimentary, my dear Watson."

---

# THE MUSIC HALL MYSTERY

My friend Sherlock Holmes was, as one may have noticed from my memoirs, not one given overmuch to light entertainment. But there were occasions when he did deviate from his more solitary entertainments and enjoyed an evening at the theatre or music hall. Yet even then his ever-active mind never ceased to resolve the most amazing problems.

It was yet another of those ghastly London November evenings, when the fog was so thick we could have been in Bangkok or Belgrade so far as one could tell. Visibility was poor. From the street outside came the normal sounds of evening traffic in these circumstances - the squeals of runaway horses, the jolly cries of the pickpockets and footpads, the ringing of the omnibus bells as the vehicles lurched over the bodies, potholes, horse-droppings and other obstacles in their paths. Mrs. Hudson had cleared away the remains of yet another of her tasteless dinners and a certain restlessness filled my friend. I sat and meditated upon the meaning of Life and continued quietly to write up some of my Notes for these accounts, whilst my friend read the 'Times' in silence, but a silence interrupted by occasional and uncharacteristic fidgeting and twitching. And then, with a cry, he flung down the newspaper and said, "Come, Watson, let us go and see some Life, hah? I confess, I feel so bored and restless that, were someone to invent a wooden box with a glass screen and stick it in the corner of the room, I would probably sit and stare at it until madness reigned. Come, let us go out and explore what London has to offer!"

London had, of course, a great deal to offer two gentlemen in such circumstances, so taking sure to check that I had my Army revolver and that my friend Holmes had his stout knobkerry, just in case, we dressed in our capes and caps and sallied forth into the gloom.

My friend seemed sure of his way and at times I had difficulty in keeping up, twice having to pause and pistol-whip an importunate beggar in order to clear a path. But we walked at some good pace down Baker Street and through the West End, my friend abjuring any thought in these circumstances of taking one of the hansoms that loomed so sinisterly out of the murk, until we came to the Strand and entered one of those brightly-lit emporia of semi-innocent entertainment known as Music Theatres.

We were almost in time for the beginning of the second show of the evening and after I had purchased our tickets we made our way to a suitable spot near the middle of the theatre, the persons already sitting in the seats we wished proving very willing to move as soon as I had shown them the butt of my revolver. Settling into our seats, Holmes took out a little snuff box and partook of a small amount of the cocaine he habitually used on those occasions when he wished to relax, and then we began to peruse the Programme.

Apart from the usual Opening Numbers and choral dancers - ladies whose costumes required the observer to possess good eyesight, if only because there was so little of them - the programme included a motley collection of balladeers, jugglers, comedians and - a Mystery Guest. This last particularly interested Sherlock who enjoyed, of course, nothing so much as a good Mystery, and so we awaited the appearance with a sense of keen anticipation.

We were not to be disappointed. With a brief roll of drums the Manager came onto the stage to announce the imminent appearance of the night's Mystery Guest. Not only that, but he announced that the Theatre Management had concocted a stimulating additional entertainment, inasmuch as the guests present on this night were all invited to guess the identity of the Mystery Guest and, following the evening's show, were invited if they so wished to visit the Box Office and submit a small card with their supposition.

109

Should any be correct, the guest in question would be invited to partake of dinner with the Mystery Guest; should more than one member of the audience have the correct answer, the first card to be received would claim the prize; the Management reserved of course the right to refuse admission, to disqualify all friends, relations, friends of relations and relations of friends of the employees of the theatre, and the Management would not enter into any correspondence regarding the prize.

Following which announcement, he bowed deeply and departed the stage.

The lights were dimmed, the curtains parted and a figure appeared centre-stage, to a chorus of gasps and calls from the audience. All I could make out, with my limited experience of such entertainments and entertainers, was that the person in question was undoubtedly of the female persuasion, but when I mentioned this to Holmes he observed, mysteriously, that even this could not be assumed certain in such an establishment. On my querying his remark, he added that there were many expert Impersonators around these days, but he then refused to explain any further what he meant. However, he asked me to provide him with a piece of paper and a pencil and scribbled something furiously in the dark.

Later, as the lights came back on and we prepared to leave, he also asked me for the loan of a Five Pound note, which of course I was glad to be able to offer my friend. Pushing his way through the departing crowds, wielding his knobkerry with some force on occasion, as I was able to observe, he was among the first to arrive at the Box Office and submit the piece of paper to the Manager standing there.

Well, I can hardly explain my gratification when it was announced to the seething mêlée that "a Mr. S. Holmes of Baker Street, London" had won the night's prize, a dinner with the Mystery Guest. To general groans of disappointment and the occasional shout of anger (or pain), Sherlock pushed his way forward once again and I did not see him again that evening. After waiting a while for the crowd to subside I made my own way back to my rooms, having to refuse many attractive offers on the way - at least, one had to assume in the fog that they were attractive offers, since visibility was so poor.

Next day I presented myself as usual at my friend's lodgings at 221B Baker Street in time for tea. Mrs. Hudson, on letting me in, warned that "Mr. Holmes might still be abed" and indeed it proved to be the case, for he was lying in his dressing-gown, half-asleep, upon the chaise-lounge as I knocked and entered. It had been, he said, a very late night and he had not returned to his rooms until breakfast-time. The 'Times' lay, unopened and unread, on the table by his bed.

I could barely contain my curiosity and excitement and after Mrs. Hudson had poured the tea and withdrawn I asked Holmes, who looked even more pale and wan than usual, for an account of the events of the preceding evening. After consuming one cup of the reinvigorating brew and pouring himself another, then lighting and puffing for a few moments into his pipe, he leaned back into the armchair into which he had moved, stirred a lump of sugar into the steaming liquid, and looked at me over the rim of the cup.

"I observed," he began, "that the Mystery Guest was a professional entertainer, but one who wished to remain unseen. But all such entertainers crave to be seen. This indicated two possibilities; either that they had in some way lost a part of their attraction, or they were in fact merely impersonating another person, and did not dare take the risk of such imitation - of necessity slightly imperfect - being recognised.

The entertainer in question sang and spoke a piece for which Miss Ellen Terry is justly famous in several Music Halls across the land; so I asked myself, why the need for such tomfoolery with darkened stages?

In the 'Times' I had just read a review of Miss Terry's latest performance in Sunderland, so I knew it could not be her. On the other hand, there is nowadays a flourishing trend in persons of the male persuasion dressing as and imitating those of the female persuasion."

"Really?!" I was shocked. "But surely this kind of thing is not normally allowed? Besides, anyone would immediately spot a man dressed up in such ridiculous costume!"

"Do you really think so, my friend?" he replied. "Tell me, how many women were performing last night?"

I had to think back a little; "There were five in that singing quintet, eight in the chorus line - no, nine counting the one who came in in the middle; then the one who sang that ballad......"

He interrupted me. "They were all men, my dear Watson. All men."

I was astounded. How could this be? I had myself, I must confess, gazed with particular interest at some of the limbs shewn to the audience from that stage and the flouncy costumes had aroused also great interest from my inner depths. But from Sherlock's tone, I knew, with sinking heart, that what he had said was true.

"This, my friend, was the hidden purpose of last night's little entertainment. Now, I also knew from the 'Times' that there is a convention amongst entertainers that no two of them may, for professional purposes, use the same name - to avoid all sorts of other confusions.

I therefore deduced that this artiste, who so shamelessly used Miss Terry's repertoire of material, would, in all likelihood, have taken a form of Miss Terry's name, perhaps by adding a further name or a central initial or some such similar subterfuge.

The answer, as I sat there in the darkened auditorium, came upon me like a flash. It was, as you saw, but the work of a few seconds to scribble my estimation of the answer to this Contest down and pass it to the correct recipients. The rest of the evening - well, the rest of the evening was most pleasurable."

"But what was the mysterious name?" I asked, my head reeling with what I had just heard. Holmes smiled, and knocked his pipe out on the dresser.

"It was Ellen M. Terry, my dear Watson."

---

## THE CASE WITH THE MISSING SUIT.

As I may once have commented, No. 221B Baker Street was, in many respects, a difficult address in which to live. This well suited my secretive and often solitary friend. The entrance was well concealed (to the extent that there are still those who doubt that such an address has ever existed) and the consequence was that the post often took a while to reach us, being frequently deposited at either No. 221 or 223 (a laundry and a milliners', respectively). In addition the succession of young urchins employed by our newsagent, a Mr. W. H. Smith, each took a while initially to locate our doorway and as these urchins were changed with depressing frequency it was not unusual for my friend Sherlock Holmes to receive his treasured copy of "The Times" only late in the afternoon. He then, naturally, had to bend his not-inconsiderable talents at great speed and urgency to his daily task of resolving this newspaper's famous Crossword Puzzle, in order to beat his brother Mycroft who, being well-placed at the Foreign Office, had of course no problem in receiving his copy more punctually and had in any case nothing else upon which to spend his time.

It was on one of these days, when my friend was sitting with furrowed brow over Clue One Across - "An Australian bird, three letters" - this had already turned into a two-pipe problem and was showing distinct signs of turning into a three-piper - that there was a hesitant knock on our door. Most knocks on our door were, in fact, hesitant since, for the reasons already explained, most of our visitors took several attempts to find the correct entrance and had usually disturbed at least two or three of our neighbours before finding the correct "bachelor apartment", as I believe it is termed. Hence, also, the frequently-asked first question: "Is this the abode of the famous Mr. Sherlock Holmes?"

Our unexpected visitor turned out to be a young lady of most pleasing appearance and demeanour. "Ah, come in," said my friend, looking up from his newspaper. "Come in, though I see you are a lady of easy virtue."

"Really, Holmes," I could not help expostulating at this ungentlemanly insult to so gracious and fair a guest. The lady, however, blushed prettily and took a seat.

"Fear not, my dear Watson," riposted my friend. "For I observe that, although she is wearing a lipstick of good quality and pleasant shade - indeed, one so good I often employ it myself - her base powder is of a cheaper variety often used by the trollops of Limehouse and Covent Garden - the kind, if you do not mind my saying so, that charge less than a Florin."

"How can you know that?" I asked, astounded.

Holmes glared at me briefly over his newspaper. "Furthermore," he continued, biting gently on his pipestem, always a danger sign in these circumstances, "Furthermore, I observe that her lipstick, pretty though it is, has been smudged in at least two different places, indicating at least two kisses with different persons, since only one smudge bears the faint but distinct marks of a hairy moustache. You will note also, my friend, that in her bag, which is now lying open, lies a packet indicating that she has purchased some product from a branch of the Apothecary's Emporium of Mr. Jesse Boot of Nottingham, an establishment notorious for its peddling of various forms of prophylactic devices formed from Gutta-Percha or the better-quality normal Burmese Rubber. I therefore take it that I have demonstrated my assertion adequately." Saying which, he dropped his eyes and returned to the vexatious question facing him on the page. "Four Down," he said. "Beelzebub. Lord of the What? Five Letters. Damnation!"

Our visitor waited a few moments, then cleared her throat. "I need your help," she said, her voice low. "I need your help, but I regret that, in my humble circumstances, I have no means of paying."

"That should be no problem," said my friend, gracious at last in his turn. Then, turning to me, he asked, with a hint of urgency, "Watson, do you have your Army Revolver?"

"Why, of course!" I replied, "But where is the danger now?"

"Let us waste no time," he declared. "Take your revolver and stand guard downstairs. We want no disturbance for at least a good half-hour. Please make sure also that Mrs. Hudson does not come up with that infernal rattling tea-tray of hers until I give you the call."

Of course I responded immediately, though I could not for the life of me see what was so disturbing my friend, normally so calm. But as I left and closed the door I turned and saw - but no, I shall draw a discreet veil over what I saw as I left, if only because that is the exact opposite of what our fair visitor was doing.

It was nearer an hour before Holmes whistled to me down the staircase. I had heard nothing save for a few bumps and some rattling in our rooms upstairs, and possibly a faint groan, and was getting rather anxious as I stood guard. But the sight that greeted me as I re-entered the room did little to reassure me. My friend was sitting once more in his armchair, but his deerstalker cap was on back-to-front and I noticed something that I had regrettably failed to notice beforehand - and which, had I done so, I should of course have endeavoured to correct. My friend's trouser buttons were not completely fastened as they should have been! To avoid further embarrassment I leaned over and placed the folded copy of the "Times" on his lap and pointed at 4 Down, whispering at him, "Flies".

"The case is complex, Mr. Holmes," said our visitor, who had now been introduced to me as Miss Violet D'Arcy, a girl of good family albeit bad habits. "I have come on behalf of my mistress, the Lady Coniston."

"Coniston?" Holmes' brow furrowed as he sought recollection. "Of the Lakes, I suppose. I am, of course, one of Lady Windermere's most loyal fans. But I do not recollect the Lord and Lady Coniston?"

But then, before she could answer, his forehead lightened. "Of course. Are they not, mmm, shall we say, of the Hebraic persuasion?"

Miss Violet blushed further. "This is true."

"Ah yes. If I recall correctly - do be a good fellow, Watson, and pass me that copy of the new Debrett - if I recollect correctly, ah yes" - he was turning the pages now - "yes, of course, as I recalled. The Lord Coniston was once, in former times, the Lord Cohen-Stein. But not, I gather from 'The Times', for several months now."

"That is correct," said Miss Violet. "My employer's husband, Lord Coniston, was until recently a man of humble circumstances, a mere Morris Cohen of Manchester. On marrying the lady who is now my mistress, Miss Lily Stein, and rising to wealth, to the extent that he was ennobled by Her Majesty, he did indeed combine and anglicise their names - as he says, The Title is the Deed. And now for several months they have lived in some state in their mansion in the Lakeland. But at heart he remains an innocent, hard-working tailor and a true patriot."

"Then do, pray, tell us," said Holmes, "what urgent errand has brought you here. It has, I presume, something to do with a missing letter?"

Miss Violet was now in turn startled. "How did you know that?" she gasped.

"A lucky guess, my dear Violet," he replied, rather familiarly I thought; "Most of my friend Watson's accounts at some point refer to a missing letter."

I had to admit, somewhat ruefully, that this was true.Miss Violet composed herself anew and began her tale.

"Lord Coniston was travelling to London from his country seat at Foxfield, on the Night Express train of the

London and North Western Railway. On arrival at that Company's Euston station he was horrified to discover that his trunk, which contained his new suit for presentation at the House of Lords, was no longer in the Luggage Van to which it had been entrusted in the care of the Guard. This was an especial suit that my Mistress had had tailored in Manchester, rather than London, for she wished to ensure that it was of a state they refer to as "Shatnez", which so far as I understand these terms, means of a specific mixture - or better, lack of mixture - in the cloth. Moreover" - and here she paused awhile and blushed prettily before continuing - "moreover, in a pocket of this suit was a certain letter in which I was mentioned in terms of endearment and affection, plus a commercial invoice for services rendered during a previous visit to the metropolis. The suit itself is of course valuable, especially to my mistress, but it is this missing letter which so preoccupies my master. Should it fall into the wrong hands - well, who knows how severe the damage could be to his reputation, to that of my mistress - who has sent me here on this errand today - and to the entire Lancashire Worsted Industry? It is imperative, Mr. Holmes, that this trunk, and its contents, be found, and without any delay!"

 Holmes leaned back in his armchair and stared at the ceiling, his hands folded together so that the fingers met at the tips. I could see he was cogitating heavily, even though his eyes closed awhile. Finally he opened his eyes, turned to Miss Violet and said, "Carnforth or Lancaster?"

 She was as puzzled as I and could not answer. Exasperated, he turned to me. "It is really terribly simple, my dear Watson," he said, using the patronising tone which I always found so offensive but could never normally bring myself so to describe.

 "Lord Coniston was travelling on the Furness Line. To get to Euston he would have had to change trains at either Carnforth or Lancaster, unless he took the 3.18pm. from Barrow which, of course, whilst stopping at Foxfield, runs through to Crewe. But the connections onwards to London from the 3.18 are so execrable as to make it highly unlikely that this would have been his mode of conveyance. Watson - the Bradshaw!"

But a half-hour later we were in a Hansom cab heading for Euston Station. Mrs. Hudson had hastily prepared us a basket of her terrible chicken patties, which Holmes threw out of the window at the street urchins as we passed. On arrival at that magnificent if confusing station Holmes lost no time in booking a double First-Class Sleeper compartment for Miss Violet and himself, explaining that, because of the danger she was in, it was imperative that he keep guard over her during the perilous journey. I was content, as an old Army man, with a Third-Class seat in a narrow compartment. As the station clock struck 10pm. the crack Night Express stormed out of the platform and up the Camden bank.

I recall little of that journey. I slept but fitfully, lurched from side to side on the ancient and economical bogies and springs employed by the self-styled Premier Line. On arrival at Lancaster Castle Station at some dismal hour of the morning I was ravenously hungry and Holmes and Miss Violet - who also appeared to have slept but little - joined me in the Station Buffet for a welcome breakfast before boarding the stopping train to Carnforth. But before we boarded Holmes, who had - I could not help noticing - dressed in one of Miss Violet's skirts and bustles, paid a call upon the Luggage Office. His face was grim as he rejoined us, the pipe not really matching his otherwise feminine image.

At Carnforth we had once more to change and once more Holmes visited the Luggage Office before we took the Furness Line train in the direction of Lakeland. This time my friend looked more pleased with the results of his conversation but divulged nothing of his investigations.

"Foxfield, change for Coniston!" The Porter's cry jerked me out of my fitful slumber, for my eyes had been drooping ever since we had departed from Carnforth. The sun was well up. Holmes and Miss D'Arcy assisted me onto the platform and we looked around the junction platforms until Holmes cried "Aaah", quietly, with a satisfied air. "Watson, stay here!" he commanded in what I considered to be unnecessarily peremptory tones, "and take good care of our friend Violet. There is, I wager, some mischief afoot! If I do not return within the hour - then we shall meet at the Station Hotel. Book a double and a single room for one night but, for heaven's sake, do not use your real name."

With this, he swept off towards the footbridge. We waited, worried, on a station bench, until the appointed hour had long passed and then made our way to the Hotel. Having booked ourselves in as Dr. and Mrs. Whitsun, there was little to do but wait.

It was already the middle of the afternoon and I was again drowsily sitting in an armchair in the small lounge, attempting with limited success to remain awake and very conscious of the presence of Miss D'Arcy and her perfume as she sat close, indeed very close to me, when I was roused by the voice of a Railway Porter at the entrance. "Luggidge fur the parsenjers frum Lunnun", he said - this is the nearest I can attempt to this thick Northern accent. The man looked slightly unkempt, had two large brown warts on his face and was bent over a two-wheeled platform trolley; he bore the serge uniform of an employee of the Furness Railway Company and his peaked cap needed brushing.

I assumed he meant us but was puzzled as we had brought but light cases. However, Miss D'Arcy gave a gasp. "The trunk!" she exclaimed, almost bounding out of her seat, "The missing trunk! Where did it come from? How did you get it? Who sent it with you? Here, my man - Dr. Watson, please give this man a shilling!"

The Porter took the shilling with a grunt which I assumed was meant to be an expression of gratitude. He turned it over in his rather grubby hands, then slipped it into his pocket. "Ohr aar," he added, "there be a nowte un orl", and with this he handed me a grubby and crumpled brown envelope. I opened it, surprised. Inside was but a single sheet of paper, bearing the crest of the Furness Railway Goods Cartage Department and smelling slightly of horse dung. The paper bore but three words, apparently in code, and three exclamation marks: "One Across: Emu!!!" As I perused the note I was surprised to find the menial sit down in the armchair I had just vacated and turned to remonstrate with him - when he took off his peaked cap and peeled a hairy wart carefully from the end of his nose. "Good Heavens!" I expostulated. "Holmes!" For indeed it was he.

Over an excellent Afternoon Tea provided by the Hotel's management Holmes recounted to us his story. "It was clear to me," he began; "that the letter, though important, was not the key to this story. For who could know of the location of this letter, and its contents, except those most concerned to keep its existence private? No; the problem was the Suit, and the Trunk in which it was contained and had been despatched. So I determined to follow its intended course from its point of origin.

The Coniston residence is, of course, not far from here. Time was short and I had but a brief time available in order to ingratiate myself with one of the housemaids but, I am glad to say" (here Holmes permitted himself a brief and uncharacteristic grin) "I succeeded remarkably quickly, and she was very forthcoming. I ascertained that His Lordship's trunk had in fact been despatched "Luggage In Advance" by a Railway Cart some hours before his own departure for the station. He did indeed, as I had suspected, avoid the notorious 3:18 from Barrow with its poor connections, and took instead the 5:21pm., changing at Lancaster. The question is, of course: To where did the Trunk go?  We listened with avid attention. He continued:

"Assuming, as I did, that this letter was not the heart of the problem, and that even my old adversary Professor Moriarty had not been involved, I had had to assume the

Trunk was somewhere upon our nation's extensive railway system. And knowing as I did that the Conistons spoke English with a distinct Hebraic accent, the question was: Where could the misunderstanding have arisen? At Crewe (you were still asleep, my dear Watson, I suspect) I spoke with two of the luggage porters on the platform and could at least understand them. At Lancaster, the Luggage Clerk spoke with, indeed, a heavy Lancastrian accent, but we were at least able to exchange words - though I regret that my costume at the time did lead to misunderstandings of a different sort. At Carnforth, however - well, at Carnforth it proved almost impossible to penetrate the incomprehensibility of the Clerk's speech. It was clear that here, where the Trunk had to be transferred from the Furness Railway to the North-Western, there was scope for misunderstandings. As, likewise, here at Foxfield itself.

Now, Lady Coniston is renowned locally for her good manners - all the more surprising for one of her breeding and Nation - and it required but a few further investigations before I learned that she had told the Cartage Driver of this local station's Goods Office to deliver the Trunk in question to the station and place it on the train to Euston. The driver, a Mr. Manglefold, regularly takes his lunchtime beer and 'bait', as they call it, at the 'Black Dog' public house on the other side of the Goods Shed. I managed there to meet him and after I had purchased for him three pints of the strange stuff they call Beer in these regions, he confessed to me what had occurred. He had asked "Which train?" and Lady Coniston, who remains unacquainted with these parts and the railway timetable, had replied, "Oh, in all fairness, I do not know, but you decide."

Manglefold accordingly brought the trunk to the station's Parcels and Luggage Office, sat with a pile of luggage labels in one hand and a paste pot in the other, and decided that he had no idea what to do - since "in all <u>Furness</u>" - the only part of the world with which he was familiar, and the only list of destinations which he had pinned to the wall in the Office - there was no village or town called "Oysteyne." A mix-up of accents, you see. So - "

"You mean?" gasped the fair Miss D'Arcy.

"Yes; the trunk was here on this station the whole time."

"Holmes, you amaze me!" I cried. "That was masterful. You have found the Trunk, the Missing Suit and, of course, the Missing Letter without which I could never, ever write an account of this day's triumphs! How did you do it?"

"It was, of course, quite elementary," he replied, with a bashful smile. "Now, did you book those rooms? Good, but there has been, I fear, a change of plan. Watson: It is now, as we see from the clock, only a little before half-past five.
We shall cancel one of those rooms. You must accompany the Trunk to London; take the 5:21 from Barrow, which will be here in under thirty minutes, change at Lancaster of course, and ensure it is delivered to the Conistons' London address in the morning. I have taken the liberty of obtaining for you the uniform of a Parcels Porter, so you shall be enabled to travel in the Guard's Van the entire way. Keep your Revolver about you, of course, but do not let it be seen unless necessary."

"And you?" I asked, feeling some concern for his safety should he stay longer in these remote regions.

"Have no fear," he replied. "It is better that you and I do not travel together. Miss D'Arcy and I shall stay here one night and travel up to London on the day train tomorrow - it leaves here at a quarter after eight and using an Employee's Pass I have already obtained First-Class tickets for us at a considerable discount. But I must retire soon to the room and remove this disguise, which is becoming in places a trifle irritating.

As I suspected, a better brand of cosmetic base powder would have been preferable. Take the Trunk now, Watson - you may use the barrow, of course, but leave it on the platform at Carnforth, you can see from the Company's insignia that it is a Barrow in Furness and should not leave this railway's system. In the meantime, Violet, I should be obliged if you could assist me in removing this rather heavy jacket and these confounded trousers."

As they ascended the hotel staircase I took my leave with a light heart, despite the prospect of yet another night of discomfort, courtesy of the London and North-Western Railway. And I am glad to say that I fulfilled my mission with no further ado. Lord Coniston was immensely grateful and wore his special suit to the Lords - he explained that it apparently had been made by members of his nation in such a way that there was no "Shatnez", though I have no idea what this meant. Some of his foreign lingo, I presume. Holmes returned alone the next evening, spoke but little, and retired after dinner to play his violin.

The Trunk with its suit and letter had been found, and we could look back with satisfaction upon another triumph for my friend's analytical processes. But, alas, The Missing Suit Case has since remained one of the standard topics for travellers everywhere, wherever they may have had to change.

..................................................

# Other books by the Author

## The Honey and the Sting

**A Study Guide for Conversion to Judaism, written with a love for Judaism and with British Humour. (JVFG, London 2016)**

Many introductions into Judaism are available, but only few teach about how to become Jewish and how to practice Judaism every day; almost none describes this from a European Progressive Jewish perspective. This book fills this gap. It is based on materials circulated under the title "Jewish by Choice" used in European Jewish congregations for several years, written by a Progressive Jewish rabbi for his students. In the appendix it contains a list of possible questions that the Beit Din may ask and some test-yourself quizzes.

# Rabbi Dr. Erich Bienheim

"Rabbi Dr. Erich Bienheim came from a small village in northern Germany, studied in Berlin, served as Rabbi in Darmstadt, then suffered the horrors of Nazi concentration camps and exile and British internment, before coming to serve as rabbi in Bradford for the last thirteen years of his life. Sadly, he left few records and no close family but Rabbi Dr. Walter Rothschild learned his first Hebrew letters from Bienheim - he was only seven when his first rabbi died - and in a way the seeds were sown for a mirror career that has led to him leaving England and serving as Rabbi in Germany. Some rabbis become famous, others do not and Bienheim was one of the latter but he served faithfully and well and deserves to be remembered, at least, as one of those who toiled in the vineyards of the Lord - even if the harvest was often but bitter grapes. This is a personal biography, written from a rabbi's perspective - and who would know better what that means?"

## 99 Questions About Judaism

Not-Quite-All You ever Wanted to Know about Judaism but were Afraid to Ask..... In just 99 Questions and personal Responses (not Answers) one cannot cover everything but one can make a good start. 99 is an arbitrary limit but one has to start - and end - somewhere. This is an updated and expanded English version of a book which has already been successful in German and Italian, written from decades of rabbinic experience concerning the questions that are most frequently asked at interfaith meetings, schools etc. concerning this mysterious and - for many - intimidating yet fascinating religion. Filled with surprises......

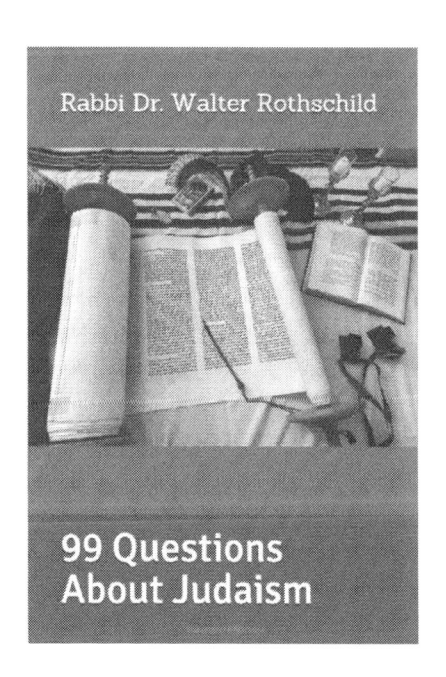

## Tales of the Chutzper Rebbe

Lost in the mists, swamps and forests of Eastern Europe, plagued by mosquitoes and Cossacks (though not necessarily in that order) lies the almost-forgotten Shtetl of Chutzp. Here is the seat of one of the lesser-known Hasidic dynasties - The Chutzper Hasidim, that mystic, anti-intellectual, ecstatic sect that placed so much emphasis on a close encounter with Hashem, facilitated when necessary through a haze of schnapps. With a tinge of nostalgia we look back at some of the founders of this Hasidic school, their disciples and others whose lives were touched by their unique view of this world and the next.

# Tales from the Rabbi's Desk

## Volumes 1, 2 & 3

As a Rabbi I had been taught always to look behind a story, to see what is hiding in the spaces between the letters and between the lines...... to be aware of other dimensions; To be sensitive, like Elijah the prophet, to still, small voices." Rabbi Dr. Walter Rothschild brings us a collection of stories, some fictional and many based on factual experiences, based on several decades of work as a congregational Rabbi in England and in Europe.

These stories give an insight into the rich tapestry of human lives that he and his colleagues have touched.

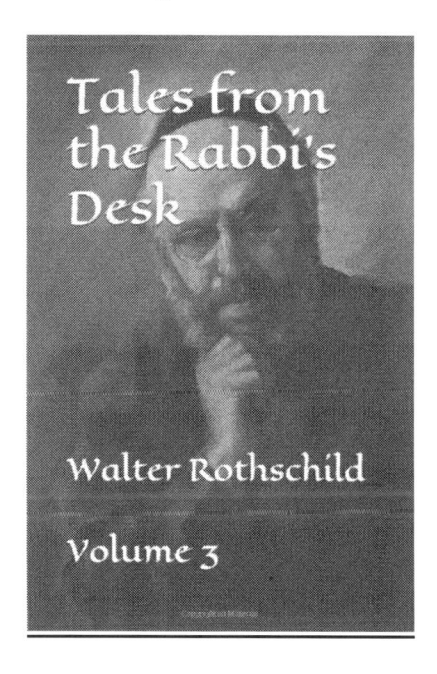

# Sherlock Holmes' Bookcase
# Volumes 1 and 2

The term 'Sherlock Holmes' has come to indicate an ascetic, meticulous observer, one whose deductive powers were useful for the detection of many a criminal and the resolution of many a literary mystery. But surely there was another side to the man, and also to his faithful companion and 'Boswell', Dr. John Watson? What sort of men were they, what were their backgrounds, what were their concerns? Over the years many have tried - with varying degrees of failure - to emulate Arthur Conan-Doyle's original writings; there are even humourless obsessives who will criticise every comma they deem misplaced. Nevertheless, we now present a new collection of stories, discovered by accident, possibly even written by accident, and designed to be read by accident. Rather than the detective's Casebook, this is more a Bookcase, mixed volumes standing side by side and on those vague borders between fiction and fantasy. The reader may explore further at their own risk.

# Cryptic Tales From The Crypt

**Memoirs of an Undertaker's Undertakings
Or: My Apprenticeship with Death.**

**By Henry A. H. Longbottom  - As told to  Dr. Walter Rothschild.**

Mr. Henry Longbottom spent some years in his youth as an Apprentice at Thistlethwaites' Funeral Directors and we are fortunate to have some recorded interviews in which he recalls some of the events of that period. Apart from keeping the premises tidy - it is the Apprentice who usually has to Brush with Death - he had to accompany the senior staff on many jobs and picked up many a fascinating tale from those who had worked there longer. These 'Cryptic Tales' are now presented by the Shadley Local History Society, edited by its Chairman Dr. Walter Rothschild.

# THERE'S TROUBLE DOWN AT T'PITCH!

Football as it really was. Memories of Huddersfax City and Cleckheckmondsedge Rovers in the glory days.

As told by a Father to his Son.

Football in Yorkshire, back in the 1920's to the 1950's – How was it really? These affectionate tales of the glory days of Cleckheckmondsedge Rovers and Huddersfax City won't exactly give the answer to this question, but hopefully they will enlighten and entertain – and may even explain a little of what went on inside the heads under those cloth caps huddled under the rainclouds in the old pictures in the papers.

## The Kreutzer Chronicles

"The Kreutzer Chronicles" written by our late aunt Irene Chavert and edited after her death by Walter, Joyce and Sylvia Rothschild is also available on Amazon. It is a novel which reflects the family history in Northern England from the 1890's to the 1930's.